THE STORY OF

WANDERING WILLIE

THE STORY OF

WANDERING WILLIE

Lady Augusta Noel

BROWNSTONE

TO

MY MOTHER

Originally published in 1870.
Published by Brownstone Books.

INTRODUCTION.

Be the day short or never so long,
At length it ringeth to even-song.

ALL DAY he had come across the moors through the falling snow.

Long ago, from some village far beneath him, the church clock had struck four, and the distant strokes had come faintly up to him, muffled by the storm. So he knew that sunset was over.

But it made little difference to him on that moorland track, except that the grey mist caught a darker tint,—that the snow-flakes looked dimmer as they fell. The great silence around could not grow deeper, or the road become more desolate and wild.

It was not desolate to him, or strange. His feet had trodden it when the purple heather was in bloom for oh! so many, many years, also the snowy mantle it now wore was not strange to him, but familiar and dear as were the silence and the twilight.

All the country-side knew Wandering Willie. Men who were growing old remembered that when they were rosy children, he used to go and come among them even as he did now. Mothers, standing at their cottage doors watching their little ones at play, often saw Wandering Willie lay his withered hand upon the golden heads and, smiling, bless them as he passed. Then they thought of the kind smile and the touch that used to be laid upon their own heads years ago, and they recalled the same simple words of blessing.

They had been waiting then for life, with its duties and its hopes—sleeping as it were, and dreaming in the golden morning-flush, until the hour struck for work. And to one after another it had come, and they arose. Busy life began for them, but to Wandering Willie no changes seemed to come.

He was looking on at life, not sharing it. He had no home he used to say, smiling gravely, as they asked him the question in the warm corner of many a happy fireside. No, he was alone in the world. But when they said 'Poor Willie,' and some kind soft touch was laid pityingly on his hand, from which the pilgrim-staff had just been laid aside, he smiled again and said he was well content.

He must be very old they thought. Each winter's snow left its reflection on his silvering hair, each autumn storm traced deeper furrows on his face. As every summer came, he bent a little lower beneath the heat and burden of the day. And in the spring there was one day—his birthday—which was ever to Willie as a milestone passed on the homeward road, as a voice of welcome from the Land that was no longer 'very far away.'

So though it seemed a restless life that he led, it was yet not a sad one. The wide sky was as his roof—the rough moorland path familiar to him as household ways. The evening brought its homely welcome—the morning its friendly words to cheer him on his way.

Not a farm-house, not a cottage in all the country round, but kept the warm corner of the ingle nook for Wandering Willie.

The children shouted for joy when they saw him coming towards their house in the gloaming. The house-mother left her spinning-wheel to welcome him on the threshold. More logs of wood were piled upon the fire. Eager hands laid his staff aside, and helped to lift the pedlar's pack from Willie's shoulder. And while he sat down to rest, the little ones danced out of doors again to watch for Father from the top of the stile, that he might come home quick to hear what Willie said, and see what Willie brought.

And then they gathered round, while the pack was opened and all its treasures spread out.

There was always something wonderful and new that Willie had brought from the far-distant town. The brightly coloured shawls—surely mother must have one—they looked so beautiful as Willie held them up; the knots of cherry ribands for the maiden's hair; the shining scissors and great horn knives, the little store of books, the tapes and cottons, and the brown duffle for the children's frocks that had been waited for so long and so impatiently.

'The mother thought thou wert never coming again, Willie,' the farmer would say smiling, as the busy housewife shook her head, and held the stuff up in the waning light and made her easy bargain with Willie.

Soon supper was ready, smoking hot upon the oaken board, and they called their guest to the most honoured place. But the pack was left open on the floor that the children might have another look at Willie's treasures.

He carried greater treasures still—treasures that money could not buy, but which were requited by the precious gifts of love and good-will.

He brought letters from the absent—kind messages from some that had been thought forgetful—greetings that were as music to loving hearts—little tokens of old friendships over which time and distance had no power. And as they gathered round him to ask questions, and listened breathlessly to his tidings, the old man sometimes spoke of joy, sometimes of sorrow, but always of comfort.

So they all loved him. But with the little ones did he chiefly seem at home. Perhaps he thought that life's journey lay in a circle, and that as the end to him grew ever nearer and nearer, he was drawing close to the spot whence the children had so lately started, and he could breathe more easily in their air, and their language came the most readily to his lips.

He would tell them stories by the hour—stories that, coming straight from his own heart, found their way at once to the child-hearts of his listeners. They loved the simple verses that he often strung together as he journeyed on alone from place to place, and they called Willie their own poet. The wise people smiled at the high-sounding name, for they thought that Willie's verses were all alike—harping only on one string. The old man said he did not know—it seemed to him as if the wind brought them to him, and it ever told one story. It may be that the children were right, and that the rhymes had a rude melody caught from the great voice of Nature—some faint echo of those solemn chords that night and day the wind sends up to Heaven, as it sweeps across the woodland and the moor towards the distant hills.

Therefore, with this music ever sounding in his ears, like distant church bells, it was not strange that solitude should be to him as a friend, not as an enemy to be shunned and dreaded. For if there be a voice in Nature that can speak to its Great Maker, surely God sends many answers back; and hourly some word of His went home with a new thrill of gladness to Willie's listening heart.

So do not pity him, though he has fought on all day alone against the storm.

Look at him now, toiling steadily onwards, a dim figure scarcely seen through the thickening snow-wreaths. At each step he sinks deeper in the snow, and all around the moor stretches wild and white under the grey heaven. Here a great broken tree rises against the sky, weird and gloomy; there a few firs are bending beneath the snowy burden that grows heavier each minute. And the falling snow swiftly fills up those solitary foot-prints that alone have ruffled its surface.

It is so silent, so very still. Who would guess that a resting place is near at hand? Yet so it is. But one more steep bit of road, and it will be lying almost at his feet.

It is hidden still by yonder rising ground, but that once gained, the moor sinks suddenly downwards, and nestled in the hollow lies the grey farm-house, where they are watching for him even now.

It is pleasant to be watched for, especially when the way has been long and hard.

Already Willie could picture to himself the ruddy gleam of light from the windows down below.

The snow-storm might blot out the outline of the house, and bury the familiar path out of sight, but it could not quench that cheery token of welcome.

A little nearer, and he should see the figures moving about in the red warmth within, and the great shadows that the firelight threw upon the ceiling.

And then close to the window-pane the waving outline of many little heads clustered together. All the children would be on the lookout to-day, straining their eyes along the darkening path, for the first sign of his coming. For it was New Year's Eve. The sun would never rise again on the Old Year. Amid the snow-flakes it was falling quietly asleep.

All day, as its last sands ran out, Willie had been thinking of the dying year and silently bidding it farewell. Rather wistfully he saw the daylight float away from it for ever. To-night it laid down the burden of its completed hours, and was fading back into the shadowy past.

But for those children in the farm-house down yonder things were different. The glad New Year's morning that would rise to-morrow from beneath the snow-white pall of the Old Year was everything to them. The pack he carried was heavy with their New Year's gifts. Willie strove to mend his flagging pace, for he was tired. He had come far, very far, to-day, that the little ones might not be disappointed.

Child-like, he rejoiced in the feathery snow-flakes that would prevent their seeing him until he was close at hand, and at the soft white carpet muffling his approaching footsteps, so that he might take them by surprise.

It all fell out as Willie had imagined; only the children were too quick for him after all. The door in the deep porch flew open as he drew near, the red light streamed out brilliantly, and little feet danced into the snow.

How many rosy laughing faces there were—how many merry voices! The children drew him in amongst them, the young ones were close to him, and the elders, just as happy, stood behind.

All claimed to have seen Willie soonest. Roger was the first to grasp his hand, and bid him welcome—Lois said so—but then Lois gave every disputed point in Cousin Roger's favour now. Besides,

Roger was so old and his legs were so long.

'We were all watching, Willie. We thought you would never come. We are so glad you have got safe over the moors in the snow.'

'And we all welcome you, old friend,' said Lois, the tall, graceful maiden, holding both his hands. 'We have so much to tell you, and Roger and I——'

She did not finish, but Roger put his hand proudly on her shoulder, and their two faces told the rest. So it was a very joyous meeting.

And on that evening Wandering Willie told them the story of his life.

He had never told that story before, and no one will hear it from Willie's lips again.

It came about in this way.

There were none but the young ones left with him. Most of them were gathered round the fire at Willie's feet. The youngest, little Cecily, had climbed upon his knee. Long ago—at least what seemed long ago to her—she had climbed up into his heart. She put her arm round his neck, and had been telling him 'secrets' in soft half-whispers. A little way off Roger and Lois sat in the window, and talked together in low voices—most likely they had 'secrets' too. The old man often looked towards them. It may be that something in Roger's attitude, or in the downcast face of Lois, brought back a dim picture to him through the far off years. He smiled, but he sighed too, as he smoothed little Cecily's fair hair. She had got his big silver watch in both her hands, and was listening to its ticking and to what Willie said about it.

The children on the hearth were forming wishes for the coming year.

'And I wish,' said one, gravely and clearly, 'that I was big, and very useful.'

The others were quiet for a moment, and then they laughed, and their laughter rang musically through the old kitchen.

Willie smiled at the little speaker, and went on with what he was saying to Cecily.

'And you see, Cecily, how the busy hands keep on and on, always doing their work. Look how quickly the long one gets on. It goes round ever so many times faster than the short one, and yet that is doing its work too all the time—doing its very best. But you could not expect the short hand to do as much, or in the world the little short legs to be quite as useful as the long ones.'

'The long ones like yours;' and Cecily held out a short bare leg of her own and looked at it.

'Yes, the long ones like mine;' said Willie. 'They have made many journeys, little Cecily.'

'Willie,' she asked, opening her eyes, 'how many times has the long hand gone round since you was a little boy?'

He shook his head gravely. The days of his years were past Willie's counting.

'Will you tell us all about it?' said the little maiden who had wished to be very useful.

Then all the others jumped up and echoed the petition. 'Tell us your story. Because it is New Year's Eve, Willie. Because it is the last day of the Old Year.'

Lois came and sat down beside him and begged too, and Roger leant over her chair.

'Do tell us about your life, dear old friend. We have so often wished to know.'

Willie still shook his head, but somehow the chord of memory had been touched to-night, and it was vibrating still. Perhaps because, as the children said, it was the last day of the Old Year.

He looked out of the window at the coming darkness, and then back upon the young listening faces in the firelight.

And he told them his story. It was a very simple one.

PART I.

We spend our years as a tale that is told

Look, it is evening, quite evening at last. See how the light has faded, and the shadows have fallen over the hills. The day is over, the twilight is gathering.

Just so it is with me. My day has long been over; the hours of work are spent, the twilight seems long, very long, but the night is at hand.

I am glad that it should be so. To the old weary eyes this dim light is welcome; to the tired frame, 'the night in which no man can work,' looks full of rest as it draws near.

You ask me how it was with me in the morning.

It is so long ago I can scarcely remember now.

In the morning, when I was young?

Let me look back through the shadowy years.

Ah yes! It comes slowly to me—the wild morning freshness, the flower-scented air. The dawn has broken; it is all wonderfully bright; there seem to be no clouds; the sun rises in golden radiance, and the earth is flooded with glory.

And as my eyes—dazzled at first—grow more used to the splendour of the young day, robed and crowned with light, I see an old gateway grim and grey, facing the west. It lies in shadow still, but a child pushes open the heavy wooden door, and suddenly a stream of sunlight pours through, and he stands there with the morning light behind him.

How often there may be two meanings in our simplest words. I was standing truly, on the threshold of life, even as my childish feet rested on the grey worn stone, and far before me lay the mists and the shadows, the hopes and the sorrows of my future. Only from behind—my home lay in there behind—from there the sunshine had never failed me yet.

My hand, a small soft round one, rested against the arched gateway, among the stonecrop and the yellow lichen. I remember that I tried to loosen one of the old stones, but I could not. It was still as strong and immovable as when, ages ago, it had been fitted into its place. I daresay it is just as firm now, though the little busy hand is so withered and feeble.

It was the gateway of a ruined castle, grand and very beautiful in its ruin. I have heard people say that they wished they could put all things back, and see it as it once was; but I always wondered at them. I would not have changed one stone.

I suppose that all places may look sad at times—beneath the grey sky of winter, or when autumn winds are blowing; but on a summer's day no place has ever seemed to me so bright with sunshine as our ruins.

It was as if old age had come upon them lightly, bringing with it no burden of sadness, and that their days of work long over, they were content to lie idle in the kind warm sun, and to tell stories of the past.

The birds built their nests in the traceried windows, and sang and loved each other, and skimmed about at their own wild will above the flowery turf.

Ivy, the child of old age, had wound itself round the broken towers, half clinging to them, half supporting them.

It was one of my mother's quaint sayings that the soft mossy grass, which grew luxuriantly everywhere, reminded her of charity, for that though Time had stolen much away, all its thefts were covered and hidden beneath that widely-spread mantle of turf.

I used to listen to my mother telling the stories of the place in her sweet grave voice. She and my father had charge of the Castle, and we lived in the rooms over the grand old gateway.

My mother often went round with visitors, for people came from afar to see the ruins. I liked to follow her, holding her gown bashfully, and wondering how mother knew that Queen Elizabeth had come there once, or that Simon De Montford, with a great army, marched up the valley one dark night and took the Castle by storm.

'Were you here, mother, when Queen Elizabeth came?' I asked her once.

'Oh no, Willie.'

'Then how do you know she ever came and stayed in the Queen's Tower?'

'They say she did,' mother said, smoothing my curly head.

'But do you believe it, mother? How can you tell if it is true?'

'Little Willie,' I remember that she answered, 'we must believe many things without seeing them,' and I thought that she looked up to somewhere higher than even the great Queen's Tower.

I thought a little, and then said—

'What a great person she must have been. Would you like to have been her, mother?'

'Oh, no, no,' and mother smiled, and then knelt down and kissed me. 'My own little son.'

I did not know what that had to do with Queen Elizabeth, and I don't know now, but I felt very sure that no queen, however grand, could ever have been like my mother. She, I thought, was more like an angel, and I believed I knew quite well how the angels look. For under the ruined roof of the Castle chapel was a sculptured angel's head with folded wings. It had just such a face as my mother's, with the same peaceful brow and loving downward look.

Sometimes I see her still. She comes to me through the long years at night, and we are together again—not as now, I so old and withered, she so young and fair—but as it used to be when I fell asleep, a tired child, on her shoulder. And I think that when the night—I mean death—really comes for me, and I lie down to sleep, that God will send her for me, and that she will take me, her weary son, in her dear arms once more.

I was an only child, but not a lonely one. On the other side of the ruins, only much lower down, close to the stream that ran under the Castle cliff, was the forester's cottage, where lived Hildred, my friend and playfellow.

It was a pretty cottage with a thatched roof, half buried in climbing roses. The pleasant rippling of the stream sounded there close at hand.

We heard the water, too, up at the gate-house, but more faintly. There it was the distant rush of the stream tumbling noisily over some rocks before it took up its quiet song again at a lower level.

The cottage garden was a sunny corner full of flowers and bees and butterflies. But we liked our grey gateway best, with its broad fair view. For we could see across to blue hills in the distance, miles and miles away. Between them and us were broad woods and broken ground, farm-houses with rich pasture-land round them, and broad fields stately with yellow corn. It was beautiful to watch the wind sweep over them with a rough kindly hand, breaking the field into waves of rippled gold beneath its touch.

I was looking at all this from the gateway on the summer morning I have been telling you of, and feeling very happy, though I scarcely knew why. For a child accepts God's gifts with a glad unconsciousness, as the earth welcomes the sun and rain.

Perhaps you wonder why I tell you so much about a day on which nothing particular happened, and why I remember it so well. But if you live to grow old, you will find out that it is not always the great events in your life that you remember the best and care the most to look back upon. It is some sunny little bit of every-day life—some homely scene that passed over and seemed to leave no trace behind, that lingers the longest in your memory. Just as looking down from a high hill at sunset over the country below, it is not the biggest things that you see the most clearly, but the bright spots here and there: a glittering pool of water, perhaps, or a bush of blooming gorse which has caught and kept the sunbeams.

You children should not have got an old man talking to-night about what happened when he was a little boy. Old men are like a great many other things, easier set a-going than stopped when they have once begun. And so I am afraid you will find me. I seem to remember so many things now that I once look back. Sad things, children, as well as merry things, for there are grey threads woven into the web of every life. I hope you will not say that mine is too 'grey' a story for New Year's Eve.

Don't be afraid though. There is nothing sad coming yet. I was as happy a little boy just then, as the sun shone on.

Little Boy Blue
Come blow your horn,
The sheep are in the meadow,
The cows are in the corn—

sang a little clear voice coming through the ruins. That was Hildred. She always sang unless she was running so fast as to be out of breath.

One day when her sister-in-law was scolding her, she said she believed Hildred began singing before her eyes were open in the morning, and that it was very tiresome. Hildred lived with her brother and his wife, for her own parents were dead.

Her sister-in-law scolded her a great deal, but she could not quite sadden the brightest little heart that ever beat. Hildred seemed to get over the scoldings as quickly as a little bird shakes off the rain-drops that have fallen on its wings.

She was sorry for a few minutes, but then she ran away to us and forgot it all. Often there were two big tears on her cheeks when she left home, but by the time she had got past the keep the wind had dried the tears, and she was singing again. She left her troubles behind and forgot them: forgot the sturdy uproarious Robin, the stolidly domineering Walter—her brother's little twin boys—forgot even that passionate blue-eyed baby Phillis, the greatest tyrant of them all.

You may be sure that my mother was all the kinder to Hildred because she had no parents of her own.

The little maiden brought all her small troubles to be cured by my mother, as grown up people brought her their big troubles. Everyone that knew my mother came to her. She had remedies for all ills, I think, from a scratched arm to a broken heart. No one went away from her without taking some comfort with them. Many people have told me this. I scarcely know it by my own experience, for as long as she lived I never needed comfort.

My father was a man of very few words. He seldom came home until the evening, and then he liked to sit perfectly silent, with his pipe in his mouth, in the chimney corner if it was winter, or in summer on a stone bench outside the door.

I was not a bit afraid of him, and chattered on to my mother just the same, whether he was there or not. I do not know if he ever listened to what she and I said to one another. At all events he never joined in our long talks. My mother taught me to look up to him and honour him, and so I did, but in a far-off sort of a fashion, much as I honoured our sovereign lord King George.

But she seemed to belong to me so completely that it would have surprised me very much if father or anyone else had set up a claim on her that came in the way of my rights.

He was welcome to talk with her, as I sometimes heard him doing, in slow deep sentences, after my mother had bidden me good night in the long light summer evening. But she was mine till bedtime.

Bed-time! how I hated the word then! How it brings back now the dear vision of a little white nest, of a few last thoughts in the waning light, of hours of dreamless sleep. Then of a glad awakening in the morning with sunshine on my face, and mother by my bed.

There was an old well under the wall that used to frighten and yet attract me, it was so very deep and dark. I always fancied that some unknown danger lurked in its depths, yet I could not resist the temptation of peering down into it, to see through all the fern and broad-leaved mulleins, the black water far below marked by one round spot of light, where the reflection from the sky touched the surface.

It was a daily pleasure to me to see the bucket lowered into the well. I took a friendly interest in that bucket, almost as if it had been a thing alive, and used to wonder whether it did not dread the rapid steady going down into darkness, and the sudden dip into the chill water at the bottom. I was quite glad when the rusty chain began to be wound up again, and the brimming bucket loomed slowly into sight.

On a stone in the wall above the well there were some words engraved in queer old-fashioned characters. When first I knew how to read, I used to try to spell them out letter by letter, but I could not manage it.

'Why can't I read that,' I asked my mother rather indignantly, 'when I can read so well?'

'The books we read now-a-days are not printed with those sort of letters,' she said, pausing for a moment in turning the creaking old windlass.

I looked down to see how my friend the bucket was getting on, and seeing him rising up safely towards me, turned back to the inscription.

'How stupid to put it so that we cannot read it,' I said.

'But wise people—people who know a great deal—read it quite easily,' said my mother.

She had landed the bucket safely on the well-side, and she stood thoughtfully, and pulled a little moss off one of the old carved letters. 'It is not that they were stupid, Willie, but that we are not wise enough to understand. Very often when we think that things are not right or wise, it is only because we cannot make them out for ourselves; but if we saw clearer and knew more, we should find out that they were only too wise for us and too good.'

She was talking to herself, I think, not to me, and I only answered the last words.

'Good; then are those old words very good?'

'Very good indeed, Willie.'

'What are they?'

She read slowly—

'For whosoever shall give you a cup of water to drink in My Name; Verily I say unto you he shall in no wise lose his reward.'

'Why, that is in the Bible,' I said wonderingly.

My mother smiled. 'I told you they were good words.'

'But how did they get there?'

'I don't know. I think some good man must have carved them long, long ago, that the water we draw up out of the well might remind us of Christ's words, and that we might remember to try and help one another.'

And then she told me how all service done for our Master's

sake—even the very smallest—should be remembered by Him, and should in no wise lose its reward.

I have forgotten the words she used, but I remember that I said, 'I should like to give some one a cup of water, mother.'

She was going back to the house, with the pitcher she had filled, but she stopped to put her hand upon my head, and answered—

'I hope you will often. Do not forget, Willie.'

I never did. That little talk, with its few and simple words, was to bring a great change over my life.

One day—it was a hot afternoon in harvest-time—I heard the bell that hung near the great gateway ring suddenly. A faint ring, as if the hand that pulled the bell was weak or afraid, but as I stood still for a minute, listening, it sounded again.

I ran to the door and opened it: a man dressed like a soldier in a faded red coat was half-sitting, half-lying on the ground leaning against the archway. Beside him, trying to support him, knelt a boy of about my own age, who looked up eagerly as I pulled open the gate.

I drew back, startled at the man's haggard face and dark hair, meaning to go and call my mother, but the boy stretched out his hand to me and said eagerly—

'Give him a little water, for the love of God!'

A little water—how strange it sounded to me—a cup of water. Mother had said she hoped I should. I rushed back to the house, seized a horn mug, and there at the well the bucket stood half full.

The boy put the water to his father's lips, and the poor man swallowed a few drops with difficulty.

'How tired he is,' I said.

The boy shook back the dark hair from his eyes and looked up at me.

'He can't get on any farther. I don't know what to do.'

'Oh, you must come in here,' I said eagerly. 'Can't he walk? It isn't far.'

The boy bent down and spoke. I scarcely think the poor soldier understood what was said to him, but at his son's voice and touch he strove wearily to get up from the ground. Between us we managed to lead him into the kitchen. He fell heavily on the oak-settle near the window.

'Is he very ill?' I asked.

'Three days ago he was struck down with fever. Last night we had to sleep under a hedge, they would not take us in at the place we stopped at, and to-day he——'

17

The boy stopped and turned round. Another voice—I scarcely knew it for my mother's, it was so changed and hoarse—repeated his words, 'Struck down with fever.'

She drew me hastily away from the sick man, whose hand still rested on my shoulder.

'Oh, Willie! what have you done—what have you done?'

'Mother, the poor man wanted some water,' I began, but she called to me to go away, and when I wanted to stay and tell her about it, she pushed me towards the door with a sort of cry—

'Go, go, I will come to you.'

I went out frightened and puzzled, and waited for her at the well.

When she came to me, I sprang into her arms and sobbed out, 'Mother, what have I done? You said a cup of water—'

I could not go on, but pointed to the stone. It was strange to see how the troubled look passed away from her face and the peacefulness I knew so well came back.

'My boy, you have done nothing—nothing wrong. I hope you will always try to follow God's commands, though it may lead you into troubles.'

'What is it, mother? Is the man very ill?'

'Very ill, Willie,' she said gently; 'so ill that I don't know yet what we ought to do. I wish father was at home. I must go back now.'

I sat down by the well and waited, watching the door. It seemed a long time that it remained closed, and no one came near me.

At last in the stillness I was glad to hear the well-known heavy knock that Farmer Foster always gave upon the gate with his stick. I went and pulled it back.

I have not said anything yet about Farmer Foster. But Foster of Furzy Nook was a name so well known in those days all round the country that it seems to me as if no one needed to be told about him.

From our windows we could see the twisted chimneys of Furzy Nook farm peeping through the trees. A quaint old-fashioned farm-house, built of red brick, standing in a hollow at the end of a long green lane arched over all the way with trees, that was the pride of the neighbourhood. To go to Furzy Nook for the afternoon had always seemed to me and Hildred the greatest happiness that the world had to offer.

Mother used to live there before she married my father, and the kind old people were almost as fond of her as if she had been a daughter of their own. Farmer Foster was always coming up to the Castle to see her.

I was very glad this afternoon to see the kind face and the gaiters and the shaggy pony looking just the same as usual.

'Well, Willie,' called out the loud cheery tones that sounded very comforting to-day, 'and how's mother?'

Holding on to his stirrup, as he rode slowly in under the archway, I told him all that had happened in the last half hour.

He gave a sort of whistle of dismay 'Struck down with fever, eh, Willie?—that's bad. And father won't be home till night?' he said, biting the end of his whip and staring at the door. 'Well, you'll have to hold the nag for me, lad, that's what you'll have to do.'

And he got off and went into the house. By and by he came out again with my mother, and they stood together talking earnestly. I was leading the pony up and down on the grass, but now and then I overheard a few of their words.

'You *must*,' Farmer Foster said once or twice.

My mother shook her head: 'I cannot turn the poor creature out to die.'

Something I heard about 'very catching,' and mother said 'hush,' and looked towards me.

Suddenly I saw the old farmer take her in his arms and kiss her. He came and took the pony away from me, telling me to go to my mother.

'Is the poor soldier better, mother?'

'No. He is very ill, Willie,' she said, putting both her hands in her old fond way on to my head; 'so ill that I must send my boy away. No, Willie, you cannot stay. Farmer Foster is going to take you home with him.'

I could not cry when I looked at her face. She was so sorry for me. I knew she would not have sent me away if she could have helped it. I pressed my two hands on to my breast and looked at the inscription over the well. My mother's eyes followed mine and she smiled. Perhaps to go away quietly from her would be more than 'a cup of cold water.'

She took my hand and we went silently to where Farmer Foster stood by the pony waiting for us.

'He is ready,' said my mother trying to speak cheerfully. 'See, Willie, the farmer is going to let you ride on his pony.'

Farmer Foster lifted me up. 'I'm afraid he will fret after you, Annie.'

'No,' she said, softly. She came close beside the pony and put her arms round me, and, as I bent down to her, gave me a long trembling kiss. 'You will be a good boy without me always.'

The shaggy pony walked steadily away with me under the gateway. I thought my mother had put her hands over her eyes, but when I turned back again, before we went down the hill, she was looking after us, and there were tears and smiles both upon her face.

That was a very sad ride. But I think it would scarcely have been in human nature—at least in a boy's nature—not to be cheered by all the joyous sights and sounds that greeted us at Furzy Nook. We got to the end of the sandy lane just at sunset, the pleasantest and noisiest time of day in a farmyard.

I tried to count the noises, but it was no good. There were too many, and all going on at the same time.

There were the cows coming home from the up-land pasture to be milked, and lowing as they wound down the narrow path. The cow-boy had a stick in his hand, which he flung carelessly among a flock of geese, and made them run cackling loudly towards their pond, where they launched themselves into the water with a satisfied splash and glide. Because the geese cackled of course the ducks began to quack. The supper-bell was ringing loudly from the farmhouse, and the bell excited the big watch-dog to rush out of his kennel and bark furiously.

We heard the distant cry of the harvesters coming from the field, where the wheat was being carried, and the creak and rattle of an empty waggon coming up the lane.

Besides that, the pigs were having a family quarrel over their supper in the straw-yard. Raised high above the noise, the pigeons cooed peacefully from their house. The rooks were floating in from the fields to the tree-tops. Then the donkey, honest fellow, made up his patient mind to have a share in what was going on, so he lifted up his voice and brayed. Louder than the pigs—harsher than the geese—more discordant than the peahen, he stood with his head thrust over a gate and made his moan to the world.

I suppose the animals all knew that the sun was setting, and were making the most of the waning day. So were the harvesters, for their cry sounded oftener—clearer, too, as Farmer Foster crossed the lane again and opened the gate into one of his big fields.

Most likely you young men now-a-days would say that he was not half a farmer. I notice that you farm very differently and I dare say you are right. Only it was not so when I was young. We did not look so carefully to every inch of land in my time.

The hedgerow trees were allowed to spread out their wide branches where they would. The ditches were often grassy and full of wild flowers, and the hedges left untrimmed. So garlands of dog-roses peeped from their sweetbriar setting. Traveller's-joy and bindweed wreathed themselves round the trailing bramble shoots. Just now the blackberries were turning from red to purple, and the furze bushes shone with starry gold.

Yet there seemed to be a pretty heavy crop of corn in the field we went into. The rakes were going over it for the last time, and the field was full of gleaners.

The gleaners had a good time on Farmer Foster's land. His people always expected, if they raked too carefully, to hear his quiet-spoken 'Gently, my lads, gently; remember the gleaners,' behind them. They said he used slyly to pull handfulls from the finished sheaves and scatter them near some gleaner, generally a child, whose bundle looked smaller than the rest, scolding it all the time for not being half a gleaner.

They were working with a will now, the level sunbeams lighting up their ruddy faces and bright-coloured aprons, and gilding the yellow wheat-ears that overflowed the bundles.

So the sun set. The lingering brightness faded from field and hedgerow. The waggons came back loaded for the last time. The heavily-laden gleaners went home singing, and the cocks and hens put their heads under their wings and settled themselves to sleep, standing on one leg.

Dame Foster and the farmer would not let me miss my mother. If I gave a great sigh they piled my plate higher with brown bread and golden butter; and once when a sob rose up unexpectedly in my throat it was stopped by such a big strawberry that I could not eat it and cry too.

And though, when I was put to bed under a patch-work quilt, in a little white-washed room that was all lighted up by the harvest moon, I am sure that my last thought was of my mother, it may be that the last but one was of strawberries and young chickens.

Every day there came to Furzy Nook a message from my mother. She was well, and sent her grateful respects to the farmer and Dame Foster, and her dear love to me. What more news the messenger brought was never told to me. I saw them whisper together and sometimes shake their heads, but as long as mother was quite well there could be nothing really wrong.

By and by there were grave faces—they still said mother sent her love but nothing more. One day, when everybody looked more serious than usual, they told me that the poor man, the sick soldier at our house, was dead.

It was very sad, Dame Forster said, very sad indeed. The farmer stroked my head and took me up on to his knee. I was very sorry for the poor soldier, but why did they look as if they pitied me?

I had begun to long to go home to my mother. For a time I tried hard to keep it to myself, because she had told me to be good without her. But I could not help asking very often if it was not time to go home. They always said 'not yet.' I got very tired of waiting.

At last Peggy told me the reason why. Peggy was a rosy, kind-hearted maid at the farm—a likely lass Dame Foster said she was, but not as discreet with her tongue as could be wished.

Peggy let out one day that I could not be taken home because my mother was ill. 'It's the fever she's got, you know, same as what the poor soldier died of. But I don't think mother's very bad, Willie dear, not like he was,' said Peggy, frightened at having made me cry. 'You must bide a bit longer here, that's all. You don't want to go away, not from the ducklings and all, do you? See, there they go! Come out and feed them, dear.'

Dame Foster could only tell me the same thing.

'She'll be better soon, please God!' That was what they said every day now.

They were very good to me, the kind old couple, who had never had anything to do with a child before.

I might have ridden the farmer's shaggy pony all day long if I had liked. He would have picked me every cherry off the tree. Dame Foster and I used to go gravely from one place to another, hand in hand—to look at the great bars of yellow butter and thick cream in the dairy—to feed the poultry, to find eggs, or to make posies of the sweet-smelling cherry pie and clove pinks out of the front garden.

One evening—Farmer Foster was out, gone I did not know where—I wandered rather disconsolately into the kitchen. It had been a long day, and it was a dull evening. The summer rain was falling softly over the garden. Dame Foster sat by the window look-ing out, and now and then putting her apron up to her eyes. I asked her what made her cry, and she said hurriedly first that she wasn't crying, and then that she supposed she felt dull with the rain and all.

I was dull too, and had nothing to do. I asked presently to go to bed, so she bade me kneel down and say my evening prayers.

Once when a little schoolfellow of mine lay sick mother taught me to pray for him and to say, 'God make Charley well, or else take him to dwell with Thee and with the angels.'

Since I had heard that my mother was ill I had added these words, after much thought, to her name in my prayers. I said them now.

There was the sound of a stifled sob behind me. Farmer Foster had come in without my hearing him. 'Bless his dear heart!' the old man said. 'The good Lord has heard his prayer.'

I jumped up from my knees.

'Has mother got quite well?' I asked eagerly.

Oh no! Farmer Foster's averted face—his wife's slow-dropping tears—Peggy's uplifted hands and pitiful, shocked look, told quite another story.

They frightened me with their silence and their tears.

'Mother!' I called loudly; 'mother!'

'Oh, little Willie!' Dame Foster said, holding out her arms, 'she cannot hear you.'

There was no need for them to tell me any more.

My mother was dead.

Who can fathom the quicksands of a child's grief?—its depth and its shallows, both so real: the passionate sorrow one hour that utterly refuses comfort, the seeming forgetfulness the next; the bitter, bitter tears, and by and by a weary peacefulness that comes like balm you do not know from where, smoothing with soft, cool touches the aching eyes and brow.

God knows the little ones are weak: He lifts away the load of sorrow now and then, lest the overburdened little heart should break, the rough stones pierce the tender feet too sharply.

I did not want anyone to pity me or try to comfort me. She who alone would have known how was gone away. They talked of my going to her some day in heaven, but that seemed too far off to do me any good.

As much as I could I kept my tears to myself, for everybody came round me if they saw me cry, and said kind things in cheerful voices, and patted me, and stroked my hair. They did not understand. If I stopped crying, as I always did as soon as ever I could, they were satisfied.

Sometimes at night it was hard to keep my sobs quite silent when I wanted mother's kiss. But directly I heard Dame Foster open the door quietly, I used to bury my face upon my arm to hide eyes that the tears made so burning. I felt the kind old lady straighten the bedclothes with a gentle hand, and heard her whisper to the farmer outside the door, 'He's sleeping nicely, bless him!' It only made me wish for mother more, who would have known all about it, and never have thought I was asleep.

Those were heavy days. Each one was long and strange like Sunday. Everybody seemed to watch me, and I felt that something, I did not quite know what, was expected from me. I walked slow instead of running, and read to Dame Foster of my own accord out of her large-print Bible.

Our few neighbours came to pay visits at the farm. I was always sent for to come and see them. They looked at me and sighed, shaking their heads gently over Dame Foster's currant wine and harvest cakes, while they talked in lowered voices about 'the orphan.'

I believe Dame Foster took a kind of pleasure in those tearful gossipings, and in going over a set of sentences that I, listening listlessly, grew to know by heart, even down to the sighs and little groans that always went with the words.

'Ah dear!' said Mistress Janet Morton, our schoolmaster's maiden sister. 'Ah dear! Here to-day and gone to-morrow, dame.'

'You may well say that, Mistress Janet.'

'The best seem to go the soonest,' Mistress Janet went on. 'There's a many will grieve for her that's been taken.'

'That's true. Everybody loved her, poor dear. My master takes on wonderful, just as though it ha' been a daughter of his own. He'll have every respect paid same as if she'd been really ours. And such a stone, Mistress Janet, as my master is going to raise to her!'

'Is he indeed? well, sure!'

'He thinks it'll be a comfort like to the dear child some day.'

'Ah! he little knows what he has lost,' said Mistress Janet, looking at me as I sat wearily on the floor with my arm round the big dog's neck.

'Poor little dear!' and Dame Foster gave her deepest sigh.

'What is the poor widower to do, ma'am, left with that young child?'

'Ah! what indeed?'

'They say he's a hard man, strange and close. I hope he'll use the boy well.'

Then they lowered their voices, and their two heads almost met across the table. So I heard no more.

Farmer Foster came home one evening with a long black band round his hat. No one told me then; I have only guessed since that my mother was buried that day.

With him was Master Caleb Morton, our schoolmaster. He had been a great friend of my mother's, and used to come often to the Castle.

Peggy was sent to bring me indoors from my usual place on a high bank among the furze bushes, from where I could look across the farmyard and the cornfields—nearly all stubble now—towards the old keep at home.

Master Caleb wanted to see me, Peggy said. I found him with the farmer and Dame Foster in the best parlour, not in the great kitchen where we generally lived. All three looked very grave.

'Willie,' Farmer Foster said, holding out his hand to me as I came near, 'Master Caleb saw your dear mother before she died, and she left a sort of message for you with him. He is come to give it to you now.'

I looked up at Master Caleb. It seemed a hard, formal way of getting a message from my mother. I had far rather—and so I think would he—have gone with him to some quiet corner out of doors, and there have listened to her last words. But the farmer and his wife treated it as if it were a sort of solemn ceremony. They sat in two high-backed chairs opposite to each other, stiff and upright as if they had been in church, and signed to me to stand before Master Caleb.

He hesitated, looking from me to them. At first he spoke just as he did in school, but presently he put his hand on my shoulder and drew me near to him. After all, the words he had to say were but very short and simple. Only just these:

'I saw your mother, Willie Lisle, the day before she died. Your father told me that she wished to speak with me. Her weakness was too great for many words, but her last thoughts and her last cares were all for you. Her death, like her life, was most peaceful and beautiful. She bade you remember the promise you made her when Farmer Foster brought you here, that you would be a good boy without her always. She had prayed God much that He would help you, and she sent you her blessing. Something she said of the day that you left her. "Tell him," the words were, "that I am glad he gave the cup of water to that dying man, and that I have rejoiced as I lay here to think how he began then to try and follow our Lord's command. All that has come of it has been for the best. Tell him how sure I am of this," and her smile, Willie, when she said that, was most bright to look upon.'

Master Caleb paused.

'I have little more to say,' he added presently, 'except this, that she left a solemn charge to you. You remember the sick soldier's son?'

I looked up with sudden remembrance. Until now I had well-nigh forgotten him.

'Before his father died, your mother had promised him that the boy, Cuthbert Franklyn, should be to her as her own child. To you she leaves the fulfilment of her promise, and she bids you be his brother. She was very earnest about this. I think she would fain have said more, but her voice failed her. Then she clasped her hands, and though I waited for her to speak again, only once or twice she whispered your name. A few hours after I left her she entered into her rest.'

That was all.

Farmer Foster and the dame pushed back their chairs and unfolded their hands. Master Caleb bent forward, and, looking as if he were half ashamed to do it, gravely kissed my forehead.

All that evening they were busy over the inscription that was to be put on my mother's tombstone. Farmer Foster had planned it all out himself, and wanted the schoolmaster's approval, for he was rather proud of his work. It was very long, as the fashion was in those days. I think now that if she herself could have known about it, fewer, plainer words would have pleased her more. I still hear the farmer's voice repeating with grave relish the last words: 'She departed this life leaving a broken-hearted husband and an only child to mourn her irreparable loss.'

Broken-hearted! Was my father really that? I wondered what broken-hearted people did, and how they went on living. I was sure I was quite as sorry as my father, and yet my heart beat just the same as usual.

Whether he were broken-hearted or not, he looked to me quite unchanged, when he came the next day, with White Billy in the cart, to take me home.

As usual he said no more than he could help, only thanking the good old people who had been so kind to me in a few gruff words, when each holding one of my hands they brought me out of the house and gave me back to him.

'He's been a very good boy,' said Dame Foster, looking at my father in a wistful kind of way, as he stood settling something that had got wrong in Billy's harness.

'I'm glad he's not been troublesome,' he answered slowly.

'He never was. Stephen Lisle'—she laid her hand anxiously on his arm—'he's but a little boy to be left without his mother. You'll take good care of him.'

'I must do the best I can, ma'am,' my father said after a minute, without looking at her.

How much afraid they all seemed to be that my father would be unkind to me. I wondered over it as White Billy trotted with us up the sandy lane. It was nothing new to me that he should drive on without saying a word. I had never been afraid of him, and I fell to questioning again whether he was heart-broken, and looking up into his face to see if I could find any signs of it. No; it did not seem as if he were thinking of anything in particular, unless it might be the pony, who had found it hard work to drag the cart through the heavy sand-track at a trot, and so had fallen back into a sober walk.

Since then I have often heard people say that Stephen Lisle was never just the same man after his wife died. Very likely they were right, and that it was because I was not old enough to read the marks trouble had left upon him that I could see no change.

I did not think about him long. The Castle came in sight. We crossed the bridge and went slowly up the hill. I knew quite well that my mother was not there, and yet my heart would beat faster and faster. Home at last, and how unchanged! The same flowerpots in the window, the roses blooming still. The door stood half open and inside the black cat sat purring in the sun.

I went in alone, looked all round, opened the door leading into the inner kitchen where I used to be sure of finding her. The flies buzzed in the window, and through the stillness the clock ticked slow and loud.

I knew she was not there, yet I called 'Mother,' under my breath, and when no one answered a terror of loneliness came over me. I rushed out of the house and round the corner, blinded by quick-coming tears. There was the well, and the bucket by the side standing half full of water just as it had stood that day.

Oh, if only I had never given the cup of water to the dying soldier! If he had never come—and yet mother's message said that she was glad.

Some one was standing at the well, leaning over it and looking, as I used to do, into the far-down water. It was the soldier's son, Cuthbert Franklyn.

I could not bear that the strange boy should see me cry. I put up both my hands to hide my face, but I suppose he saw the tears trickling through my fingers, for I felt his hand touch mine, and heard him say 'Poor boy!'

In a minute—I don't quite know how—my arms were round his neck. We were very little fellows then, but we have loved one another ever since.

Cuthbert's eyes were full of tears.

'Somehow it seems as if it was all my fault.'

'How could it be your fault?' I said sadly; 'you could not help it.'

'Oh! I am glad you think that. I wanted you to come back, that I might see you again, and thank you for being kind to us that day. And I wanted to say good-bye before I go away.'

27

He held out his hand.

'Going away?' I said, taking it, and looking up at him, for he was rather older and taller than I was, 'are you going away? Where to?'

'I don't quite know; father's friends were all dead and gone when we got home to England.' His lip trembled, and there was a shadow of trouble on his brave bright face.

'Why do you go away, Cuthbert?'

'I suppose I must not stay here always,' he said simply.

'But you may: haven't you heard? My mother said you were to be my brother.'

Cuthbert looked up eagerly, and the colour came into his face. 'But your father.'

'Wait for me here a minute.'

I found my father chopping up logs of wood in the wood-shed.

'Father, Cuthbert Franklyn says he must go away.'

I had to repeat this twice before I could make him hear; when he did, he only said, 'Well.'

'But father, he needn't go.'

'Where is it he wants to go to?'

'He doesn't know; he thinks he isn't to stay here always; you won't let him go, father?'

My father took the hatchet up again.

'It's no business of mine; I've no call to stop him if he wants to go.'

'He doesn't want to go; he has got no home, and mother said he was to be my brother.'

'I don't know how that may be,' my father said slowly.

I was thunderstruck. 'But mother said so, and you promised, father.'

He looked at me.

'I made some sort of a promise may be, as I would have promised anything then, to keep her quiet.'

He sighed, and drew the back of his hand across his eyes—the only outward sign of sorrow I ever saw him give.

'Then Cuthbert may stay.'

My father made a few strokes at the wood without answering. At last he said, 'Look you, Willie; it's a great deal to ask of a poor man.'

'Are you very poor, father?'

He stopped a minute.

'They call me close, but I reckon there's not many of them would do a thing like this; it's too much to expect.'

'For mother's sake,'—I felt, rather than knew, that this was my best chance.

'You let me alone!' he said roughly.

I waited with my eyes fixed upon him, for two or three minutes. He went on with his work; then came a sort of short laugh.

'They preach so much to me about being good to you: why am I to take in another mouth to feed?—a great growing lad too, that'll take the bread out of your mouth, most likely.'

'Oh, father!'

'Be still; can't you? I hate to see the boy about the place. He's brought nought but bad luck to me and mine.'

I thought of Cuthbert waiting for me; I thought of mother's charge to me, so solemnly given and received. I was almost in despair. If I had understood my father better, I might have guessed that he would say less had he been entirely decided and at ease in his own mind.

'A promise such as that binds no one,' he muttered presently.

Another long five minutes passed—log after log of wood was cut and thrown aside. My hope was almost gone, when suddenly my father laid down the hatchet and turned round.

'See you here, boy; it'll be the worse for you if I do this; you'll have to fare rougher, and there'll be less for you to get. You'll have to be content without so much schooling, and you must work harder.'

'Oh, I don't care, I don't care!'

'Humph.'

'Then Cuthbert needn't go?'

'Have it your own way.'

'But he may stop with us?'

'I suppose he'll have to, leastways as long as he behaves himself.'

I hardly waited to hear him to the end, or to thank him. I dashed out of the wood-shed.

Cuthbert had not moved from where I left him. He was watching for me eagerly.

'It's all right,' I shouted, rushing up to him; you're to stay and be my brother.'

He drew a quick breath, with a half-uttered 'oh,' and then, seeing my gladness, he began to smile.

And so my coming home was not all sad.

* * * *

The good my mother meant to do to the orphan boy was returned in tenfold blessing to her own child. Truly as brothers—more than as brothers, if it might be—Cuthbert Franklyn and I came to love each other.

He who had never had a home before, got to be at home with us. It was very pleasant to him, though to me it seemed all changed and dreary. Hitherto his life had been a wandering one, following his father's regiment wherever it went. He was not born in England, but in the Island of Malta, and sometimes, when the sky was very blue, he said it recalled to him a brighter sky still, which he remembered dimly, and tall white buildings, and stairs that he thought went right down into the sea. There were sounds of bells and guns, he said, and a vision of some great ships. That was all he recollected of his birth-place. His mother had died there, and another soldier's wife had taken care of him. They went from place to place, sometimes taking long voyages across the sea, until his father became ill and got his discharge. When he came back to England he tried to find his relations, but his parents and his only sister were dead. He was forgotten, and could find no one to befriend his son. Cuthbert scarcely knew where his father had meant to go, when the fever came upon him. That was all he could tell us about himself; only there was no life like a soldier's, Cuthbert said, with sparkling eyes. He was always whistling the gay tunes that their band used to play, and imitating the bugle-calls that he had known all his life long.

My father scarcely ever noticed Cuthbert. To the end I do not think he grew really to like him; but his word once given, he would not go back upon it.

In time I almost forgot, and so I think did Cuthbert himself, that he did not belong to the place as much as I did.

The neighbours wondered very much at my father's having taken in Cuthbert. It was not a bit like Stephen Lisle, everybody said, to do such an out-of-the-way thing. Perhaps it was not; but I believe most people do something that is not a bit like themselves once or twice in their lives. My father heeded them very little.

He could never make shift to get on, the neighbours further said, all by himself, with two boys to look after.

That was true enough. He pondered over it in his silent way for many a day, and at last he made up his mind.

Late one evening White Billy came slowly under the archway, and in the cart beside my father, who had been away for a day and a half, sat a little old woman, with a very big black bonnet and a red cloak. My father called me.

'Willie, here's your grandmother.'

And the little old woman got down slowly from the cart, and

said,

'Dear, dear! Is this your boy, Stephen?'

'Yes, mother.'

The name sounded strange from my father's lips, strange and sad too, for he used to call my mother, 'mother.' It was odd and perplexing to me altogether, that my father should begin to have a mother just when I had lost mine. I stared hard at my grandmother. She had come to stay, I soon found out,—come to take care, my father said, of me and of the house.

'And of Cuthbert,' I said, jealously.

My father only nodded, but that was consent enough to satisfy me.

My old grandmother took possession quietly and humbly enough. The morning after she came I found her looking out over the ruins with rather a forlorn expression on her gentle old face.

'Do you like the Castle?' I asked her.

'I don't know, my dear, I don't know. It looks an outlandish tumble-down kind of place. I never saw any like it.'

'This was the great gateway,' I said, with a child's eagerness to teach anybody a great deal older than himself. 'There used to be a draw-bridge here once.'

'Dear, dear!' said my grandmother not understanding the least, 'was there indeed?'

'And yonder's the keep. They kept all their stores in there, you know, grandmother.'

'Well, to be sure!'

'And the dungeons are underneath, where the prisoners used to be.'

'Lawk a' mercy, poor things!'

'And grandmother, you've heard of the Queen's Tower?'

'No, my dear, I know nothing at all about it.'

'But you'll have to tell the people when they come to see it,' I said anxiously. 'Mother always did.'

'I can't, my dear. I know nothing of the place.'

'But you'll learn, won't you? I will teach you.'

'My dear, I am a great deal too old to learn.'

She looked quite frightened and confused. I shook my head and said no more. I did not see how she was to get on at all, and I thought how very different people's mothers could be from one another.

Years afterwards I understood good old Granny better. When she was very old and feeble she used to tell me—Granny was always fond of talking—about the little home she had left to come and keep house for her son in his time of trouble.

'It was a nice clean little place, Willie,' she would say, twirling her thumbs and looking round her with eyes that had grown very dim, 'clean and very cheerful—just half way down the street, my dear, where you could see everything that was going on. It was a tidy street; we all kept our doorsteps so clean, you could have eaten your dinner off them. We took a pride in it, you see, Willie. We were very sociable and friendly among ourselves. I could always pop on my pattens and run in next door, or next door but one, may be, for a word of chat and a dish of tea. I had lived there a long time, and we were very comfortable, you see, Willie. It seemed a bit lonesome just at first, when Stephen brought me here. But it's all for the best, my dear, all for the best, for sure.'

I could understand then, what I used to wonder at as a child. It must have been a change from the busy county town, with its orderly trimness and sociable ways, to the wild silent ruins on the hill-side. But she had come away willingly from her cosy home, at her son's bidding, and I am sure she died without ever thinking that the sacrifice so simply made was anything good in her.

By degrees I got used to seeing the bent figure trotting about, where my mother used to move; doing her work—not filling her place—keeping the house beautifully clean and tidy, but for the rest—ah, it would always seem empty and blank. There would always be the sense of something wanting.

Granny won my heart, though, by one thing. She was always kind to Cuthbert, just as kind as she was to me. I believe she took him as a matter of course. We were both strangers to her, he not much more than her own grandson. Besides, Cuthbert's bright face and ways won her heart. 'The boy has such a pretty tongue,' she used to say. He welcomed her more readily than I did, for he could not compare her, as I was for ever doing, with my mother.

I told Hildred one day how good Granny was to Cuthbert.

'Perhaps she likes him best,' Hildred said, throwing an apple up into the air and catching it.

'Oh, do you think so?'

It was a new thought to me. I pondered over it a great deal when I was alone.

Very likely most people would like Cuthbert best. My mother of course, would always have cared for me the most, but now it was different and I should not be first any longer.

Cuthbert wondered why I went up to him that evening and put my arm over his shoulder. He was hard at work mending a net for our cherry-tree, so he only just looked up and nodded.

No wonder everybody liked that happy face of his. In truth, I think there could not have been happier children than we were.

As the quick months and years passed over our heads, the trouble that never could be cured kept gliding away, further and further back into some very far-off past, until at last it seemed to me that it was not I who had lived here with my mother, but another boy, a much smaller, graver boy—a better boy, too, perhaps—but very different from what I was now. I looked back at him half wonderingly, half regretfully, through a sort of mist of brightness and light. It must have been so easy for him to be good alone with his mother, and hearing nothing day by day but her good words. What would she have done with the big rough fellow that had grown by degrees into her little boy's place? Would he have been quiet and gentle enough for her, if she had lived? Yes, all the time I felt a sort of certainty that she would have loved me, nay, that she did love me still. And I should like to have let her know, that though of course I had got into a harder life—a life in most things far unlike what it used to be when she was with me—yet that I still often remembered and wished to obey her words, that I should try to be good without her always. But these thoughts I never spoke, even to Cuthbert.

I was a child when Cuthbert came, I was a boy now, and he had helped to make me one. From the first time I saw him climb the outside of the Queen's Tower, swinging himself upwards from branch to branch of the old ivy, he became my pattern: I resolved to follow him, and if it made Granny scream to see us, why, so much the better.

The Castle ruins were the best play-ground that children ever had. On half-holidays the whole school used to troop up there directly they were let out, and the old walls rang with shouts and laughter. Cuthbert and Hildred were always glad to see them, but I liked it best when we had it all to ourselves.

There was a hole in the wall, through which we used to creep, a steep bit of cliff to climb down, and then the stream. Across it such woods, green, tangled, thick with brambles and underwood, full of wild strawberries, blackberry bushes, rabbits, and birds'-nests built up in the huge trees that stood knee-deep in king-fern.

Wherever Cuthbert and I went, and we went everywhere, little Hildred tried to follow us. It was clearly understood that she was never to be in the way. 'Girls always were,' Cuthbert said loftily; 'but still'——It would have been hard to leave her at home because she was a girl, for she would so fain have been a boy. She might come, if she would scramble through the brambles, without caring how much she scratched her arms and legs, and tore her frock. She must be ready to cross the stream, even if the rains had swollen it, and it was sparkling away ankle-deep over the stepping-stones.

She must not scream, however high a branch one of us fell off when we were birds'-nesting. She must share in all our scrapes, and never tell. She must stifle her terror of robbers in the wood, or adders in the long grass, and her pinafore must be always ready to hold birds' nests, eggs, young squirrels, or any prizes that we could not stuff into our own pockets.

Hildred was well content to come on any terms, and ready for the roughest expedition—readier often than I was, for in hot weather, when the ruins were sunny and silent, I liked better to lie on the grass reading, than even to go ratting with Cuthbert and our dog Trusty.

I was half ashamed of being fond of reading. No other boy was, and Cuthbert could not understand it at all.

'He's wonderful fond of his book is Willie,' Granny used to say. 'He'll get to reading to himself by the hour together.'

Cuthbert shook his head with a kind of wondering sorrow. He never cared much to go anywhere by himself. So there was nothing for it but to throw the book into the window of the keep, and go off wherever Cuthbert had made up his mind to take me. And there was Trusty too, with tail upright and eager eyes, waiting for a start. It would have been hard to disappoint Trusty.

He was a dog indeed, was our Trusty, commonly called Rusty, because the wear and tear of life had made his black coat very shabby and brown in these latter days. He was not a model dog, not brave, and calm, and wise, like the dogs one reads about in books. Rusty had his foibles. He was vain, touchy, and changeable. His temper, too, was apt to be short at times, yet how true-hearted and faithful he was to those he really loved! Oh, dear old Rusty, laid to rest now, for nearly fifty years, under the green grass, I have never seen anything like you since!

Who so quick to guess your mood as Rusty? Who so ready as he for a bit of fun? Who so willing to deceive himself and you, and to growl savagely or bark shrilly at the mere mention of a rat, that he knew quite well did not exist? Who so sober and wiselike as Trusty, if you were in trouble; but who so quick to mark the first lifting of the cloud, and to know the minute when it would do to break in with a wag of the tail and a short sharp bark inclining to cheerfulness?

'Come, old fellow, things are not so bad after all,' he has often said to me; 'don't worry, but come and see after that rabbit under the

Castle wall.'

To say that everybody was fond of Rusty would not be true, for the worst parts of his character came out with strangers. He was uncertain to them, uncertain and ungrateful. I have known him form friendships one day and be ashamed of them the next. He sometimes went so far as to receive kindnesses from strangers, and then to fly at their legs if he saw one of his own people coming. But to those who lived with him he was just perfectly loveable. I don't think I can say more than that. He and we loved one another.

So Rusty shared all our fun, and all our troubles too—such as they were—for we had our troubles of course; who hasn't? For instance, we hated school, at least Cuthbert and Hildred did, and I, wishing to be like them, said, and I believe thought, that I hated it too.

But I don't think I did; no, I am sure I did not, except when the sun streamed hotly in at the half-open door, and leaves tapped against the diamond-paned windows, and bees hummed past out in the warm air, and the boys were rebellious, and the girls sleepy and cross. Of course no one could like it then. Nor on a grey day just made for fishing, with cool shadows lying on the water. Cuthbert began grumbling, on such mornings, before his eyes were well open, at the hardships of having to be shut up in school all day. It was rather hard certainly to think of the river swirling along through the green rushes, eddying round the stepping-stones under the Castle cliff, or dreaming lazily over the shallows where the trout lay. I never looked up from my slate on a day like that, without expecting to see Cuthbert's place empty, and his cap gone from its peg near the door.

It was no good giving him advice—no good begging him to be industrious: he always promised, and always meant to keep his word.

All the seasons were alike. Long before I had had time to rejoice at birds'-nesting being over, the fishing had begun. Then came summer, with its long hot days—the hay-making and the bathing in the cool stream. Every bright hour was a temptation. After that the harvest seemed to come upon us quickly. The holidays began, and I had peace.

But winter was almost the worst of all. How Cuthbert loved the frosty weather, and the snow and ice! The Castle looked marvellously solemn and grey, rising out of the snow; and we had to dig paths for ourselves across the ruins. When we were building a snow man in the Castle court, and there was sliding and skating going on at the mere, half a mile away, and the red sun set over the hills at four o'clock in the afternoon, how was any one, said Cuthbert, to find time for school? 'When the thaw comes, Will, I'll never miss again,' he promised. But the snow melted, and there came a cloudy day with a southerly wind, and Cuthbert was off half-a-dozen miles away to see the hounds meet, and to follow them from covert to heath, and from field to common, all across the country.

Those lawless doings of Cuthbert's disturbed me very much. I always felt as if he were in my charge and I had to answer for him.

Our schoolmaster used to frown, and tell Cuthbert he must take the consequences; and the consequences Cuthbert took, with a great show of not caring, laughing at Hildred because she could not help crying, and comforting me as if I had been the one in trouble.

Now and then my father spoke a few rough words, but they did not weigh much, for Cuthbert said: 'It's not as if he heeded whether I got any learning or not. It's all one to him. I can see that plain enough.' And when my father had done speaking he would go off whistling carelessly. I have seen the tears in his eyes, though, for all his whistling.

If mother had only lived it would have been different. Some of her kind grave words would have set everything straight. What could poor old Granny do beyond holding up her hands at him, with her favourite 'Dear, dear!' and then giving him a double share of dumpling at supper to cheer him up?

'Boys ought to like school, Cuthbert,' she told him.

'But you see I don't, Granny. I hate it.'

'But good boys are fond of their book. Look at Willie.'

'As if I should ever be like Will,' he answered, with a look as if he were proud of me.

'Master Caleb thinks all the world of our Willie,' Granny went on. 'Why, you might go a-walking out with him if you were good, like Willie does.'

Cuthbert made a wry face. 'I'd much sooner not, Granny, thank you.'

From the time I was a little child I had known Master Caleb Morton well—he came so often to the Castle. It was he who had told my mother all the stories she knew about the place. He loved it almost better than we did, and—we were very proud of that—he had written a book about it, a real printed book. He gave it to mother, and it stood on our book-shelf, between 'Pilgrim's Progress' and the 'History of Jack the Giant-killer'—a thin red book, with a woodcut of Wyncliffe Castle on the title page.

Cuthbert and I believed that a stone could scarcely fall from the crumbling walls without his finding it out. He used to stand for hours with his hands behind his back, gazing up at the grey towers.

Poor dear Master Caleb! He was much too good for us at Wyncliffe; for he was very clever, very learned, very hard-working, and understood everything under the sun, except village boys and girls.

They baffled him, for he expected them to like learning, and never could make out why one and all treated him as an enemy when he wanted to teach them their lessons.

Years ago he had come a very young man, to be schoolmaster at Wyncliffe, full of grand plans, and thinking to make good scholars of at least some among his pupils. He might well have found out, long since, what a hopeless task it was; but when I went to school, he was working away, still eager, still hopeful, forever being disappointed, but never quite losing heart.

However, if he did not know how to keep order in the school—and some people said he did not—I verily believe he knew everything else in the world.

He was an Antiquary, I have often heard Mrs. Janet say, and a Botanist, and a Geologist, and an Astronomer. The words sounded so very grand as Mrs. Janet rolled them slowly out, that I recollected them all, though I had not the least idea what any of them meant.

'He's too book-learned for us, that's where it is,' the great men of the parish sometimes said, shaking their heads wisely. Yet they were fond of him and proud of him all the same.

Mrs. Janet shook her head too. She would fain have ruled Master Caleb's scholars for him, as when he was a little boy she used to rule himself. It was pain and grief to her to sit idle in the parlour, and know that 'the boy' was letting things go their own way too much in the school.

Not that he always did so by any means. The boys said they never knew what he would be at, for they found themselves brought to justice now and then when they were least looking for it. There was a boyish corner in his own heart, staid, quaint, and learned as he was, that gave him a secret fellow-feeling for Cuthbert's love of roaming, and I guessed that he was oftentimes the hardest upon him when he was most tempted to let him off altogether.

With the youngest class of all—a helpless cluster of tiny boys and girls, who were only sent to school because they were in the way at home, he was at all events tireless and gentle. Very tenderly he guided the fat forefingers to point along the lines, helped the lisping baby tongues over the hard words, and never lost patience with the blue, wondering, foolish eyes that could see no difference between

A and Z.

It was when he turned back to the first class, great boys who could learn and wouldn't learn, that the puzzled, worried look we all knew well came across his face. I think the reason he was so good to me was that I really liked to learn.

So he lent me books, and took me for long walks across the hills. Wonderful walks they were—very different from the headlong way Cuthbert went across the country. Master Caleb carried a hammer with him to chip off bits of rock, and a trowel to dig up out-of-the-way plants, and a big basket to carry what he called his specimens. He loved the beautiful earth with a great reverent love.

I think Master Caleb must have been very lonely, or he would never have made a friend of such a boy as I was; but for all his learning he was just as simple-hearted as a child.

Even I knew more of the world than he did, at least of the world as it was at Wyncliffe. He came at last to treat me as if I was nearly his own age, and to talk to me of the things that he was thinking most about.

For Mrs. Janet, proud of him as she was, rather disapproved of his learning. She could not well say what harm she expected it to do him, but she was clear in her own mind that Caleb went too far. He knew so much and saw so many sides to everything that he got mazed, she said.

'But there is more than one side to most questions, isn't there?' he sometimes asked.

'Yes, Caleb. There's a right side and a wrong, and that's enough for me.'

'Well, my dear,' I remember her saying eagerly to him one day, when it was so hot that everything and everybody had gone wrong in school, and the sound of a scuffle had reached her from afar; 'Well, brother, I trust you haven't spared the rod to-day.'

'Why, Janet,'—he pushed back the hair from his forehead,—'it's very hot, and everybody feels cross. I'm sure I do.'

'Caleb!' in an awful voice.

'Don't you believe in atmospheric influences?' asked Master Caleb, who was rather fond of bringing out a hard word now and then.

'Atmospheric nonsense,' said Mrs. Janet, knitting furiously.

He stood at the open door watching the great thunder-clouds that came marching across the sky to the battle. Cuthbert and I had not gone home to dinner because of the coming storm, the first heavy rain-drops of which were beginning to fall sullenly.

'To talk of such-like heathenish things,' burst out Mrs. Janet presently, 'before your scholars too.'

'Heathenish things—electricity. I will prove to you——'

'Boys,' she went on unheeding, 'the weather is always good weather, and no one ought to feel different in hot weather or in cold, or whether it rains or the sun shines. No, Caleb, I don't care what your books say.'

For Master Caleb had brought a big heavy book from the shelf, and after rubbing the dust off the leaves with loving care, was laying it open on the table before her.

The mere sight of it scattered his enemies quicker than any of his arguments could have done; Cuthbert seized his cap, and was through the door out into the rain in the twinkling of an eye.

Mrs. Janet suddenly remembered that the pudding needed her instant presence in the kitchen. Master Caleb and I were left alone.

'It's all in here,' he said, looking up at me with a baffled face.

'What is, sir?'

'The Laws of Electricity. It's no good talking to women—to most women, that is to say. See how clearly he puts it.'

I don't know whether it was the thunder-storm; it may have been the atmospheric influences (what hard words) that made me feel so stupid. I looked at the big book with a sigh. 'Did one man write all that, sir?'

'Ay, that, and a vast deal more. It was written, Willie, by Professor Bruce.'

No wonder he spoke the name in an impressive under-tone. It was one very familiar to all Master Caleb's friends. Professor Bruce was his hero. Professor Bruce was seldom out of his mouth. According to him, Professor Bruce had written something to prove everything that could be proved. Master Caleb's one boast and source of pride was that he knew the great man well. Several years ago Professor Bruce—now growing old—had left London, where he had passed most of his life, writing books and lecturing, and to the everlasting glory of our quiet old town, Morechester, he had lived there ever since.

It was the greatest honour Master Caleb could bestow on me, the only one of his many kindnesses that he ever thought deserved my gratitude, that a time came when he deemed me worthy to see Professor Bruce. It was on the day of the thunder-storm that I knew my good fortune first.

'You're a hard-working boy, Willie, and the sight of a great man like that will do you good. I'll take you into Morechester.'

'To Morechester, Master Caleb! will you really? I've never seen a town before.'

'You will see Professor Bruce,' he answered sternly.

'Oh yes,' I said hurriedly. 'Professor Bruce of course. I meant that. Thank you, sir.'

So it was settled.

Master Caleb, good man, need not have been so sharp on me for wishing to see Morechester. It was not only to visit Professor Bruce, as I found out afterwards, that he cared so much for going there himself.

'Cuthbert, I wish you were going too,' I said just before we started.

'I should like well enough to go to Morechester,' he answered, stretching himself, 'but I'd rather not see any more schoolmasters.'

Market day at Morechester! The busiest and most stirring scene I had ever beheld.

A long sunny street stretching up a hill, built of irregular houses,—old and new, tall and short, brown and grey and red,—high houses with square windows and green shutters,—short houses, having high-pitched roofs, carved wooden balconies, and queer-shaped windows overhanging the roof; here and there a gilt weathercock flashing in the sun; oaken pillars supporting the jutting-out upper storey of some quaint old house; shop windows full of gorgeous coloured stuffs; the grey town hall, rich with ancient sculpture, standing back within its own railings; bright light, and black shadows lying across the uneven pavement. This, then, was a town.

Further on, the street widened into a sunlit market-place, and there an ever-shifting crowd came and went, bought and sold and bargained, round the old market cross.

What a noise there was! Farmers were riding up the street in twos and threes; their scarlet-cloaked wives jogged along laden with baskets of eggs and fresh butter; clattering carts, horses for sale were being trotted up and down, loud voices talking all at once.

Above all this there floated suddenly the music of airy chimes, followed by three slow deep strokes.

'Three by the Minster clock,' said Master Caleb.

The house we stopped at was close to the great towered church, which seemed to overshadow it and push it into the corner. It was a little low house, with dormer windows in a thatched roof, standing further back than its neighbours, and quite out of the reach of any stray sunbeams that found their way over the Minster roof.

Master Caleb rang a jangling bell, and as we stood waiting,

whispered hurriedly, 'Make your bow, Willie, and don't speak unless you are spoken to.'

We were inside in a narrow passage; then a door opened.

'Hush,' said Master Caleb.

I never saw any room at all like the Professor's study. Coming into it out of the sunshine it was at first too dark to see anything distinctly. The only window looked out upon a blank wall. Inside, the walls of the room seemed to be made of books, and there were piles of them besides, heaped up on the chairs and on the floor.

What wonderful things there were crowded on to the tables and mantel-shelf, and filling the half-open cupboards. Wonderful things? frightening things rather. I am not going to describe them, seeing that I know not what any of them were. 'Chemical apparatus' is the name Master Caleb gave them afterwards, whatever that may be. But such a number of queer-shaped jars and glasses, and saucers and tubes, such odd glass spoons and ladles, such strange liquids and powders, and bits of metal as were lying about, I should think no one else ever gathered round them before or since.

My first thought was, whatever Granny would say if Cuthbert and I made her clean kitchen at home half so untidy-looking as this.

Then I saw the great man himself sitting at the table holding an open letter in one hand and an oddly-shaped bottle in the other, an old man with a keen wrinkled face, who seemed to me at first sight to be all black and white; for white eyebrows shaded his piercing black eyes, and he wore a black velvet cap over his white hair, and a black dressing-gown, against which his long thin hands looked wonderfully white.

He seemed too eager over his letter and his bottle to have much time to spare for greeting Master Caleb. He began directly, speaking fast and loud. To my surprise Master Caleb immediately got excited too, and stood listening with a rapt face while the Professor poured out a torrent of hard words. I don't think it was English that he talked, or I should have understood it. After that I did not need to be told what a great man he was. I had heard it for myself.

My best bow was not needed. No one noticed me. I sat down, as Master Caleb had bidden me, in a corner, on the edge of a chair that was piled up with big books, and listened with respectful wonder. But the hard words I did not understand went on for a long time, and the room was hot, and full of odd sleepy smells. I much fear that I fell asleep in Professor Bruce's study. Once I woke up for a minute with a great start, and saw Master Caleb on his knees, pouring something into a saucer, while the Professor shouted directions at the top of his voice, and there was a fizzing noise and an odder smell than ever.

Then I dozed again, but was roused by Master Caleb's jumping up suddenly, and turning back the sleeves of his coat in a great hurry. The Professor looked up impatiently. 'What's the matter?'

'I think somebody is coming,' said my master. The Professor listened for a minute. 'Why, it's only Dolly,' and went on with the reading of his letter.

A door behind his chair opened quietly, and there came in a small, lame girl in a grey gown.

This was 'Dolly,' then, and that was what I thought her at first, just a small lame girl in a grey gown. 'Dolly' came in slowly, and Master Caleb turned round and made her a beautiful low bow. He tried to go and meet her, but the Professor had got his hand upon his arm, and was pointing to him with the glass tube, and evidently had just come to the very pith of his discourse.

Dolly—Mistress Dorothy, as I called her later—leant over the back of her father's chair, and smiled at Master Caleb. Watching her from my dark corner, I presently saw how good she looked and how her eyes lighted up her pale face when she smiled—nice soft eyes they were; just as grey as her gown.

Professor Bruce never found out that his listener was not as attentive as before; but I saw more—his thoughts had wandered away from the wonderful saucer since the young lady came into the room.

I was getting tired of sitting so very still on the edge of the big books. I wanted to hear Mistress Dorothy speak. She saw me too, for she looked full into my corner, and then glanced at Master Caleb with another of her pleasant little smiles.

We waited until the Professor folded up the letter, and turning round in his chair so as to look up in his daughter's face, said, 'So we have got it all right at last, Dolly.'

She said heartily, 'I am so glad, father,' and then everybody moved.

The Professor pushed back his chair and stood up.

'Caleb Morton was in luck,' he said with a pleased look, 'to come in just as I was reading that letter. It makes it clear, Caleb, doesn't it.'

'Indeed it does, Professor. Mistress Dorothy,' and he went a step or two near to her and spoke low. I just caught the words, 'ventured,' 'my best boy,' and 'Wyncliffe Castle.'

She came to me with her hand stretched out. I made the bow that had been waiting for so long and at the first word from her clear voice I felt as if we were friends.

We had tea before we went away, in Mistress Dorothy's parlour, which looked out upon the Minster, and was so near to it that when the bells chimed the quarters it sounded as if they were ringing in the room itself. It was because this was a town, I supposed, that there was no sunshine, and everything in the room looked brown or drab or dark grey.

Mistress Dorothy looked very happy, notwithstanding, and not at all as if she thought the room dull. She took me to the window, where her chair and the table with her work-basket stood, and showed me how she could see through one of the side windows of the Minster, to where another great painted window facing the west was blazing in the sunset.

'Is it not beautiful?' she said.

There was a shimmer of gold, and red and blue, but so far off.

I wished she could have seen Farmer Foster's field of sainfoin as it was just now, a glittering rose-coloured sea, that looked in the evening light as if some of the sunset clouds had floated down to earth.

Mrs. Dorothy could not even see the sunset; the Minster towered between her and the red-gold west. Poor little Mistress Dorothy! and yet she looked so happy, so cordial and contented.

By-and-by she began to ask me questions about home. The Professor had gone back to his study, and Master Caleb stood in the window opposite her chair.

'Have you got a father and mother?'

'No; he has lost his mother,' Master Caleb answered for me; and then rather abruptly he began to tell her about my mother's life and death. He told it in beautiful words, that made me listen as if it were a story about some one I had never known.

Mistress Dorothy clasped my hand closer in her own as he went on, and looked down to hide, I think, the tears that were in her eyes.

'And so she died,' ended Master Caleb, 'and the boy was left to grow up as best he could.'

There was something in his voice that made me look up at him—something I could not understand.

Mistress Dorothy must have known better what he meant, for she answered softly—

'And yet it was best so.'

Master Caleb bowed his head gravely. 'No doubt you are right, Mistress Dorothy. Only it has often struck me as a strange answer to the promise that whoever gives a cup of water shall in no wise lose his reward. The boy did his best, and where is his reward?'

'We do not know yet,' she said, 'but it will surely come. Master Caleb, you are a schoolmaster; do you always give your best rewards in schooltime? Don't you often keep them to the end, when your scholars are leaving school to go home? Perhaps Willie will wait for his reward even until then.'

'You are speaking of the next world, Mistress Dorothy,' he said.

'Yes,' and she turned to me. 'You will be content to wait, Willie?'

I answered 'Yes' then, because I thought she expected it of me.

With my whole heart I say it now.

* * * *

'Well, Willie,' said Master Caleb, when he had walked a long way on the road home without saying a word, 'so you have seen him.'

'Yes, sir; it was very surprising to hear him talk.'

'Ah! he's a wonderful man.' He spoke as if he scarcely knew what he was saying; and then, waking up again, 'a very wonderful man.'

'And oh! sir! don't you like Mistress Dorothy?'

'Like Mistress Dorothy—I should never think of such a thing—don't talk of it—like her, no.'

'Oh, I thought you did.'

'I am surprised at you, Willie,' he said, and would not talk any more; so we went home silently, through sunset and twilight and moonshine.

I went a long way across the hills next day, in search of a certain fern that only grew in one place. It was a very rare one, Master Caleb had told me, a soft feathery thing, that I fancied might please Mistress Dorothy. I carried it home and waited anxiously, hoping that Master Caleb would take me with him again to Morechester. But he went alone, and Mrs. Janet said she could not think what ailed him that he was always on the tramp.

My turn came again at last, and I carried my fern to offer to Mistress Dorothy. She looked quite bright and pleased as she took it from my hands.

'I should never have thought of bringing it to you,' said Master Caleb.

He did not add what he had told me on the road, when it was too late to turn back, that it was not near good enough to give to her.

But I think she liked it. She took me into the parlour to see her water it, and made me tell her about the steep bank where it had grown, under waving trees and among primrose tufts.

'Pretty place,' she said smiling.

'Won't you come and see it some day, Mistress Dorothy?'

'Father cannot get away, and I never leave him.'

'Couldn't he spare you?'

She shook her head. 'Oh no, never.'

'But supposing you married and went away?' I asked.

I do not know what set me on thinking of marrying just then.

She coloured and smiled.

'That will never be. I could not leave him; and besides, no one will ever want to marry a little lame thing like me.'

'Won't they?'

She shook her head again and laughed.

That evening, as we walked down the street, Master Caleb said suddenly, 'She likes you, Willie; she says you are to come again.'

'Does she? Oh, Master Caleb, shouldn't you like to have her there at home, and let her see the Castle and all?'

He put his hand on my shoulder, and said in a low, changed voice, 'If it could be, Willie, if it could. But it never can be—never.'

'She says she cannot leave her father.'

'It isn't only for that; I could never ask her. Look you, Willie; she is just as high above me as the stars.'

That was how I came to know Master Caleb's secret.

* * * *

It was a heavy secret to him, poor fellow, though he tried hard to put it away, and to live as if he had not got it on his mind. He told no one, not even Mrs. Janet, and only sometimes, when we were out on the hills, he talked a little of it to me. Certainly I was a very odd person for him to have chosen to hear the story of his love. But he had lived a solitary life, and perhaps his telling me had been an accident at first. Once told, no one in the world could have felt more honoured than I did, or have listened and looked on with more reverential awe.

'You're not quite like a boy in some things, you know, Willie,' he once said to me. 'Besides, she likes you.'

And he never did things just as other people did. I suppose that was another reason.

Mistress Dorothy and I became firm friends. I did not wonder the least at Master Caleb, for there was no one at all like her in the world. To go to Morechester and see her, I gave up willingly the best cricket match of that summer; and what boy can do more than that?

The game, played on a certain sunny half holiday, was just beginning, when Master Caleb and I set off for Morechester. I remember looking back wistfully at the ground, and seeing how smooth and inviting it looked in the sunshine. The players were just crossing the field for an 'over,' and Cuthbert was walking by himself rather sulkily, for he and I had quarrelled that morning about my going so often with Master Caleb.

He said that I did not care for cricket any more, or for him, or for anything but poking about after the schoolmaster. His injustice stung me deeply; for, to tell the truth, long walks with Master Caleb were not the same things now-a-days that they had once been. He had taken to stalking along in a brown study, with his hands behind his back, and I, carrying the basket, had to follow silently behind. I would fain have been somewhere at home with Cuthbert, only I could not tell Master Caleb so.

'If you only knew all,' I said rather grandly to Cuthbert, and then stopped short, afraid of letting out the secret. Cuthbert laughed scornfully, and I walked another way. So we had quarrelled.

The little house in Minster-yard became quite familiar to me. I almost wondered why Master Caleb cared to go there so often. His visits must have given him more pain than pleasure, for he generally left me to talk to Mistress Dorothy in the parlour, while he shut himself up in the study with the Professor. Anxious as he was about the safe-keeping of his secret, from no one did he guard it more carefully than from Dorothy herself. He was always fancying—most needlessly—that she was on the point of finding it out. And then of course she would never speak to him again. So he rarely said much to her, but listened with strained attention to her father's discourse, when he would have given the world only just to sit still and look at her.

Then, when he had scarcely allowed himself a look or a smile, he went home with a heavy heart to his hard work, and tried to throw himself with all his might into spelling-books and the multiplication table.

It was an odd life that Professor Bruce's little daughter lived, in the dark rooms among the books. She rarely saw anybody except now and then some old friend of her father's—some one just as learned as himself, who came to Morechester for the day, to talk over a scientific question with him, and who paid Mistress Dorothy grandly-worded, old-world compliments about her 'sweet eyes,' and her 'dishes of good tea.'

But in general she and her father were alone. He adored her, and left her to herself. If 'Dolly' was not within call to give her ready help and attention the moment he needed it, the Professor was impatient and disconcerted. Yet even she was not suffered to interrupt him in his work. She read his books, talked to him on his favourite subjects, guarded him jealously from being disturbed, and kept her own thoughts to herself. The world of dreams she lived in, full of noble thoughts, and lofty hopes, and brave self-conquest, he did not know much about.

He was contented if she were near him, always bright, quiet, and helpful, with the quick eyes and the ready wit that never knew weariness in his service. Her father did not know, and she herself scarcely guessed, how entirely he had grown to lean on her.

This was something of what Master Caleb told me about her, when, very rarely, he broke the silence of reverence with which he held her in his heart.

Why it was that I never saw her without wishing to be braver and better, I did not understand myself. But so it was. How the stories she sometimes told me, with the light in her eyes and a thrill in her quiet voice, made my heart beat with a great longing to do some great thing; how some of her words, simple and quiet as they were, have been with me to strengthen me in all the battles of my life—nay, how they are with me still, it would not be easy to explain.

'I can't think what you talk to her about,' said poor Master Caleb, almost angrily, sometimes. 'I can never find anything that seems good enough to say to her.'

It was but too true that he did not shine in her presence. Even I, used to his odd ways, and satisfied that all he did must be right, often wondered at his long silences and awkward speeches.

It seemed so easy to talk to her, nay, so impossible not to be drawn on by some magic in her way of listening. Voice, laugh, her changing face, the quick answering smile, her very attitude, all showed her ready interest.

All this time the Professor worked on happily at his chemistry and experiments, took up more of Master Caleb's attention each time that he went to visit him, good-naturedly called him his promising disciple and fellow-worker, and never found out how the disciple's interest flagged sometimes, and how difficult he found it to give his full attention.

Nevertheless, his admiration and devotion were just as great as ever, and Master Caleb would have been covered with remorse and shame at the mere notion of finding any hour long that was spent in the Professor's study.

By-and-by also, there came a certain happy time when he began to feel that he was really making himself useful. A new book of Professor Bruce's was going through the press.

There were few prouder men than Master Caleb, as he helped to gather together the scattered sheets, to go over calculations, and to get the pages ready for the printers. Dorothy, too, to make the work doubly pleasant, was always in her father's study, writing from his words, finding, as nobody else could, the papers he was for ever losing, and helping heart and hand at the finishing of the work.

'My last book, Dolly,' said the old man, putting his hand fondly on the head that was bending so intently over some of his crabbed writing. 'I shall never write another.'

Dorothy looked up at him quickly, and tried to make a cheerful answer, that did not seem to come readily.

'No,' he went on, rather as if he was thinking aloud; 'no, I shall never write another. Perhaps already I have writ too much. But I am glad of this one, because it is well sold, and will help to make Dolly comfortable when I am gone. I've never done enough for her heretofore.'

Dorothy looked up again, and laid her hand softly on his arm, glancing from him to Master Caleb, who was frowning over what looked like a long sum, and then at me, as I stood near the door waiting for some papers I was to carry to the post.

By-and-by she brought them to me, and followed me out into the passage, shutting the door behind her.

'Is this all, Mistress Dorothy?' I asked, as she looked thoughtful.

She turned round quickly. 'Thank you, Willie; yes, that's all. I don't see you often now,' she went on with a smile, 'but he likes me to be always with him; and do you know, I can't bear to be ever away from him. I cannot quite tell why.'

'Dolly,' called her father's voice, with the softness all gone out of it, sharp, short, and impatient. 'Dolly, who has touched the index? I can't find it.'

She ran back into the study, with a nod and smile to me.

So as no one wanted me at Morechester, I did not go there for a while, but stayed at home with Cuthbert, and mended up the old quarrel of a year ago, that he had never quite forgotten. We played at cricket in the glowing June evenings, until the long shadows faded quite away, and the blue of the sky darkened into purple.

People are rather apt to lose count of time in the days of haymaking. Everybody is so busy. We did not go to school then. Early and late Cuthbert and I were in the fields at Furzy Nook. Farmer Foster wanted to have all his hay carried by the last days of June. 'And after that there'll be school beginning again,' said Cuthbert, with his old disconsolate look.

We were leaning over the stile on Sunday evening, looking at the half-cut hay-fields, with their cocks of sweet-smelling hay. 'By-the-by, Will,' went on Cuthbert, 'what made Master Caleb look so solemn to-day? He went hobbling away through the churchyard as if he had been a hundred.'

'Did he?' My heart rather smote me. It was so long since I had seen him or thought of him, and to-day I had followed Farmer Foster out of church by the door that led across the meadows to Furzy Nook. 'He's been away at Morechester but I'll run over now, and ask after him.'

Master Caleb was not under his cherry-tree watching the sunset as usual. He was indoors, sitting with his back to the window, holding a book open in his hands. Mrs Janet, with a thorough look of Sunday leisure all about her, sat very upright at the table, reading also.

'I thought you were at Morechester, Master Caleb,' I said, as he looked up and held out his hand.

'Oh no. I came home a week since. Well, Willie, how's the hay-making getting on?'

'Pretty fair, sir, if the rain keeps off;' and I looked anxiously out of the window. I knew that there was not the shadow of a cloud to be found anywhere, and no chance of rain; but Farmer Foster always scanned the clouds when he was asked after the hay; so it was probably the right thing to do. Master Caleb nodded absently.

'Is the Professor's book done yet, Master Caleb?'

'Here it is.' He held the book he had been reading towards me.

'Printed and all!' I turned admiringly over the pages, some of which I must have carried to the post myself when they went to be printed. 'Did he give it to you?'

'She did.'

His hand trembled as he took it back. Cuthbert had been right in saying that he looked worn and ill. It seemed a trouble to him to answer questions, and I, having the fear of Mrs. Janet somewhat before my eyes, could not think of anything to talk about.

'Master Caleb,' I said, after standing near him for a few minutes, hoping he would speak, 'when you see Mrs. Dorothy again, will you tell her, with my respects——'

He interrupted me. 'You can tell her yourself, Willie, when you go to bid her good-bye. Ah, you haven't heard. They are leaving

49

Morechester.'

'Mistress Dorothy? But not for long?'

'I mean that they are going away altogether.'

'Going away! where to?'

'To live in Scotland.' His voice sank a little.

'Oh, Master Caleb!'

He looked across at his sister, and half smiled.

Great rough boy as I was, I nearly burst out crying. I stammered, began to say I was sorry, and had to stop short.

He put his hand kindly on my shoulder, and presently he said, 'There is just a chance of their not going, Willie. It was not finally settled—just a chance.'

'It's quite as good as settled,' observed Mrs. Janet, without looking up.

'I know it is.'

'Why, why do they?' I asked, finding my voice at last, but with a sort of crack in it.

'Because they want him to be Professor of Chemistry at some place in Scotland, if you must know everything,' said Mrs. Janet, answering again, to my surprise. 'That book you have there is very much thought of, and he is Scotch, and so he wants to go—There!'

'But Mistress Dorothy?'

'She is sorry,' said my master, in a low voice.

And then the silence came down upon us again. Mrs. Janet cleared her throat, and held up her book so as to catch the remaining light, and Master Caleb leant his head upon his hand. I durst ask no more questions. But when I went away, he came out with me into the garden, over which the twilight was beginning to gather.

'I am very sorry, Master Caleb,' I took courage to say then.

'I know that you are, Willie.'

Quiet as he was, he spoke with a sort of effort, as if each word gave him pain.

'Scotland seems so far off.'

'Yes,—we shall see her face no more.'

'Is she very sorry? I am sure she does not want to go.'

'She said she had been happy here, God bless her. But I hope—I think—that such an one as she is must always be peaceful and happy. May He keep her so.'

'But Master Caleb, what will you do?'

He did not answer for a minute.

'I am thankful to have known her. My star of light. She has been to me——'

That sentence he never finished.

The following day ended the week that Professor Bruce had taken to consider whether he should accept the appointment offered to him or not. Master Caleb could not rest without going to Morechester to learn his determination, and in obedience to a message from Mistress Dorothy that she would like to see me again, he took me with him.

On the way to Morechester we talked ourselves into a hope that the Professor would have decided not to go away. The cool bright touches of morning air, full of the song of birds and of the smell of dewy flowers and freshly cut hay, made us feel hopeful. We remembered how Professor Bruce had said that he should write no more books, because he was growing an old man, and this new work would be harder still than book-writing. Master Caleb felt sure that Dorothy was afraid of it for her father.

'Depend upon it,' he said, 'we shall find that he has listened to his daughter, and will rest content with having had this great honour offered to him.'

After that I was astonished at the silence that came over him as we walked up the High Street of Morechester. The freshness of early morning still rested on the town, the shadows from the east reached right across the street, and few passengers were stirring except people coming in from the country, carrying fragrant baskets of vegetables and fruit.

'We shall soon know now,' I said. 'See, there is Mistress Dorothy.'

She was coming out into the sunshine through the great door of the Minster, among a little knot of people that scattered in different directions. We came up with her as she stood on her own doorstep.

'Willie,' Master Caleb whispered hurriedly, as we crossed the market-place, 'do not say a word about our being sorry. We must not trouble her. It would grieve her good heart to think it gave us pain.'

'But she will stay—you said so?'

He shook his head.

Dorothy turned and came to meet us. 'It is kind of you to come over,' she said, trying for her usual cheerful tone, as she went before us into the little parlour. 'You wished to hear our fate. Yes, it is settled, the letter will be sent to-day.'

'And it says——'

'That he will go.'

Master Caleb bowed his head. 'Of course,' he said in a low voice.

He went to the window, and stood looking out for a moment or two, while Mistress Dorothy spoke to me; but how he managed the smile with which he turned back directly, I cannot think.

'Then I wish you and the Professor all happiness and success, and—you will not quite forget old Morechester.'

'Never,' she said earnestly. 'Master Caleb, indeed this is not my doing. It frightens me for my father. I don't think he is looking well. But he has so set his heart on going, and if I say a word against it, he only says, "Let me go home, Dolly, let me go home." I thought he had forgotten Scotland, but the old love for it seems to have come back. I cannot keep him from what he calls his home, or try to make him stay here.'

'No, no. To be sure not. Why should you?'

'I should have been so glad. But that does not matter, if only it is good for him. He is tiring himself already, making preparations.'

'Then it will be soon——'

'I suppose so. And since it has to come, the saying good-bye, the leaving here, and all the rest of it, it had better be soon over.'

'Yes,' answered Master Caleb, breaking out into one of those unlucky speeches that said one thing and meant another, 'it'll be a blessing when you are gone.'

She smiled a little. 'I think it will. And for you too. I know you will be sorry.'

'Oh, never mind that. It doesn't matter much for me,—I mean, don't think—It doesn't matter, I mean——'

'I am afraid you will miss my father very much.'

'Oh yes, your father. Of course I shall miss *him*. Everything will be gone that I care for in the world,—the chemistry, you know, and all.'

'And my father will miss you. Won't you come and see him?'

She went across and opened the study door. The room was all in disorder, drawers open, book-cases half empty, and their contents scattered about all over the tables and floor.

The Professor, with more colour than usual in his face, was moving about, adding something every minute to the confusion. He stopped with a whole shelf-full of books in his arms, as Dorothy said cheerily, 'Father, here is Master Caleb Morton, come to wish us joy. Why, dear father,' she added, half laughing, 'what are you doing to the room?'

'There's no time to lose, my dear, and a great deal to be done. You are welcome, Caleb Morton, I am obleeged to you,' as Master Caleb offered his help. 'Yes. I shall be very grateful for any help that will enable us to get away more quickly to my future post.'

'Dorothy cannot comprehend,' he went on, as Dorothy was called away, and he gave up the books he held to Master Caleb, and sat down in his arm-chair. 'She does not see any occasion for haste. But there is no time to spare; I am called upon to fill an important chair.'

'I was not surprised, though very proud to hear of the honour tendered to your acceptance, Professor,' said Master Caleb.

'Ah, well, it is gratifying; yes, doubtless. You were a true prophet about the book, it appears, Master Caleb, eh? But I do not dwell so much on that. It is poor Dolly's good that is actuating me now. I think of Dolly's future and of the time when I must leave her. I should like her to be comfortable then. I have laid by but little for her at present, and I shall be glad to be getting more.'

'If the exertion be not too much,' said Master Caleb, doubtfully.

'I do not fear it; my mind is made up.' He was looking tired already, and passed his hand once or twice across his forehead. 'It is only the hurry and trouble of this move that worries me, and the having to think myself of every single thing. Dorothy has no experience. But you must not keep me talking,' and he got up restlessly; 'I have no leisure for that. Where is Dolly?'

She was coming back.

'Just look about for the list of the books, child. I had it but a moment ago; things get mislaid, and I have got to go over it.'

'Here it is; but father, you need not tire yourself with that, dear.'

'Dolly, leave me to manage my own concerns. You have no experience. You had better pack up your clothes, my dear. That is your business. Well here, if you want something to do, just go over the books on the lower shelves. I cannot stoop any longer.'

There was no chance of farewell words from Mistress Dorothy that morning.

* * * *

It was but a few days after this, Master Caleb sat at his high desk in school, the evening sun was creeping slowly across the benches towards him. Already it shone in two gold square patches on the white-washed wall. The hum of voices was growing a little louder as the moment of release drew near, when a man in a smock frock, with a long whip over his shoulder, looked in at the open door. Every head was raised to look at him and everybody knew him—the carrier from Morechester.

'It's just a message as I promised I'd give Master Caleb,' he began; 'old Mr. Bruce's young lady, in Minster yard, you know———'

'Yes, I know.'

'Ah! She sent her kind respects, and thought you'd like to know as how her father's dying. Yes, its some kind of a stroke or a fit,' the man went on, untying a knot in the lash of his whip, and answering the questions Mrs. Janet put to him from the window. Master Caleb had got to the door and stood leaning against it saying nothing. 'He was took last night, they told me, close upon nine o'clock.'

The rows of faces along the room were some of them indifferent, some looking on carelessly, others were bent down again over their books, but each one lighted up with unmixed pleasure when Master Caleb said in a hoarse voice, 'The school is dismissed, children.'

And the schoolmaster was gone. For many days afterwards, Mrs. Janet sat in her brother's place. The school was quieter than usual. The boldest hearts quailed a little before the upright figure at Master Caleb's desk. No one looked up or whispered, without feeling the quick eyes upon them, or saw with entire composure the hand that often strayed towards the tawse, that lay at her right hand. Many were the low-spoken lamentations over Master Caleb's absence; hearty the wishes for his speedy return among us.

But I believe he had forgotten all about the school, forgotten everything outside the quiet house in which his old friend lay dying. Very quiet it was, and silent. The rooms had fallen back into their old order. All token of preparation for a journey had vanished; none such was needed for the solemn journey on which the master of the house was bound.

He had been busy and earnest about the arrangements to the last. Dorothy told how constantly his thoughts dwelt on the future, and how he would spare himself no exertion in his restless longing to be gone, and at work in the new sphere. He was always hopeful and eager, and could not bear her to notice how tired and over-taxed he looked at times.

On the last evening, as he sat alone in his easy chair, he seemed to be trying to put words and sentences together, and repeating them half aloud. Dorothy did not dare to vex him by interrupting him. As she stood out of sight behind him, she heard, with a vague feeling of fear and sadness, that he was preparing the first lecture he meant to give when he got to Scotland.

The words did not come easily. He sighed and appeared perplexed, pressing his hand wearily upon his forehead, and once after a pause she heard him say, 'for Dolly's sake,' and patiently begin the broken sentence over again.

Then she could not keep silence any longer, but came round and leant over his chair to speak to him. He looked up at her wistfully for a moment or two, and held her hand. 'Dolly,' he said at last, in a whisper, 'What is it? am I too old?'

She only said 'Father.' She gathered him in her arms, and held him nearer and nearer to her; she drew his head down upon her shoulder. What they thought of, those two, as they rested there heart to heart, while the twilight sank down over them, will never be known to any but themselves and God.

Later in the evening, when it was quite dark, she left him to get lights and to make him a cup of tea. She was away but very few minutes. When she came into the room again he had sunk back in his chair, and his head had fallen on one side.

There was never any hope, though after a day or two he seemed to be getting better. His mind was quite clear, he knew everybody, but was too weak for many words.

Only one thing, they said, was strange. He had entirely forgotten all that happened just before his illness. The hopes that were so keen, the cares that weighed so heavily, he never referred to again. Not a single fear for Dorothy ruffled the serenity of his thoughts.

He smiled at her, smoothed her hair feebly as she knelt beside his bed, and sometimes kissed the little hand that ministered to his wants. But the untroubled look was very strange to those who had watched of late the gallant struggle with his failing powers that he had fought through for her sake. Now he was leaving her alone, and he did not even remember it.

'It is such a blessing, such a mercy,' Dorothy said, twisting her hands tightly together, her only sign of emotion. She looked calm, but there was no room for any thought beyond the moment itself—her father's hourly need of her, his sleep, his waking, the words of peace with which she tried to drive away the cloud that sometimes darkened over him, like a shadow thrown back from the days of his long life. 'So many years,' he used to say sadly, 'so many, many years.'

Once only I was allowed to go into his room. Dorothy had been called away, and she bade me stand by the door ready to go for her the instant she was wanted.

Like a picture I can recall the scene now. The darkened room—orderly and quiet—the narrow bed against the wall, on which the Professor lay—beside it the figure of Master Caleb bending forwards with a heavy book open upon his knees, the only book that was near at hand now—all the others had been taken away.

He said the world's learning was over for him, its learning and its wisdom, and so by degrees Dorothy had moved all the books quietly away, and left the Bible.

Master Caleb was reading to him now. The Professor had asked for some words that, half-remembered, kept sounding in his ears, and Master Caleb finding them, read them aloud. Sad words they seemed to be, whose burden was vanity and vexation of spirit—weary words, that told how all things are full of labour, and he who increaseth knowledge increaseth sorrow—strange words to read beside one who had learned so much, but who was going now to his long home, for the silver cord was loosened, and the pitcher was broken at the fountain.

'And further, my son, by these be admonished,' read Master Caleb slowly; 'of making many books there is no end, and much study is a weariness to the flesh.'

The reader's voice sank lower and lower; the mournful words sounded like autumn winds sighing through leafless trees. He ceased, and the book sank upon his knees; still the sad echo, 'Vanity of vanities, all is vanity,' went floating through the room.

The dying man sighed heavily. 'All true,' he murmured; 'the dust shall return to the earth as it was,——'

Then his look changed. Some one had come into the room softly as Master Caleb read, and was standing behind his chair. It was Dorothy, and there was a smile on her face that made her beautiful.

She took the Book out of the hands that had dropped it, turned over the pages quickly, and began to read. If you have ever heard music change from long chords of wailing sadness into a burst of triumphant harmony, if you have seen the sun break from behind a cloud, you have known what we felt then.

'Behold, I show you a mystery,' she began.

Yes, a greater mystery than any that their earthly labour could bring to light, even the mystery of immortality.

She did not raise her voice as she went on, but all through it there thrilled the glorious faith and triumph of the thought that 'death is swallowed up in victory.'

And as she uttered the solemn thanksgiving to Him who giveth us the victory her father spoke again.

'Thanks be to God,' he repeated after her, raising his hand feebly, and in the silence it seemed as if the Conqueror Himself drew nigh, and stood by the dying bed.

* * * *

The great bell of Morechester Minster was tolling heavily, each

56

slow stroke falling upon the ear like a blow, and the blinds were all drawn down in the little house under the shadow of the Minster tower when Caleb Morton came home.

He left Dorothy, as she wished to be left, alone. The faithful old woman, who had been for years their only servant, was taking care of her. For the rest she was better by herself, now that the watching was ended, and the life-long blank and sorrow begun.

After he knew that it was her wish to be undisturbed during those first bitter days, Master Caleb was hardly willing even to enter Morechester, lest she should hear of it by some means and think that he had been unmindful of a wish of hers. But his heart yearned over her, and either late at night or in the very early morning he ventured secretly now and then to the back door of the house to ask for tidings of her.

The great question that was for ever in his thoughts was this: What would Dorothy do in the life that lay before her? Her father had said truly that it was but very little he had to leave her. His one brother, the hard-worked doctor of a poor Highland parish, was scarcely likely to be better off than he had been.

To him, however, her only near relation, Dorothy had written, and till the answer to this letter came, she would fain let the future rest.

That answer was very slow in coming. The posts to the north of Scotland were tardy and uncertain at that time. Days had grown into weeks since the Professor's funeral, and still we waited. One evening, however, old Susan answered Master Caleb's low knock at the kitchen door with unwonted quickness, scarcely waiting for him to speak before she thrust a letter into his hand. 'Just you read it for yourself, Master Morton; I brought it away without Mistress Dolly's knowing of it, on purpose for you to see it. Some one ought to know how they treat the poor lamb.'

Master Caleb tore it open, without stopping, in his eagerness, to consider whether he had a right to read it or not. The letter was not long. A formal condolence on the severe bereavement she had sustained; a regret that he and his only brother had never been enabled to meet again after their long separation,—a hope that she found herself as well as could be anticipated under the melancholy circumstances, and at the end, a half-expressed chilling invitation to make his house her home until, as no doubt would be the case, she could enter into some permanent arrangement better suited to her.

'What did she do?' asked Master Caleb, looking up with blazing eyes.

'She just fetched a long sigh,' said the old woman, 'a long, long sigh!' and she put the letter into my hands, and said, 'See, Susan; he does not want us.'

Master Caleb had meant to stay in Morechester that night, and had left me, as he sometimes did when he was away, to sleep at the schoolhouse.

Mrs. Janet and I sat up rather late that evening. She was sewing, and I, on my best behaviour, was reading 'Baxter's Saint's Rest' aloud. We were both thunderstruck when the door opened suddenly, and Master Caleb appeared, dripping wet, for it was raining heavily, and looking as pale as death.

'Caleb! you here!' exclaimed his sister, getting up in astonishment to meet him. 'What brings you home on such a night as this? why, how wet you are!'

'I am come,' Master Caleb said, disregarding the hand she laid on his drenched coat-sleeve, 'because I cannot bear it any longer—because I want your counsel—because she is left all alone, and has no friend—no friend in all the world but us!'

'You speak of Dorothy Bruce,' said Mrs. Janet, slowly.

'She is so lonely,' he went on unheeding, 'and I want to comfort her, but I do not know how, and I cannot tell how to help her. Janet, you must tell me what I can do for her—not because she is alone, and that I pity her, but, Janet, because I love her.'

There was an instant's pause, and then his sister threw her arms round his neck. 'I know it, Caleb,' she said, with a great sob, 'I know it; oh, my boy, did you think I did not know it all the time?'

And as she held him in her arms, and kissed his forehead as if he were indeed still 'her boy,' I stole away and closed the door upon them.

Master Caleb came to me early the next morning, and bade me get ready to go back with him to Morechester. 'I am going there again,' he said, 'and if anything occurs, which is far from likely, to detain me, I shall be glad to send you back with a message to my sister.'

He was very quiet. All the hurry and excitement of last night were gone, and in their stead there had come over him a look and manner of grave calmness and resolution.

'Last night, Willie, I told my sister Janet what my feelings have long been; Janet said she knew already,' and Master Caleb paused for a moment in renewed wonder. 'I really am at a loss to conceive how, but so it was. And she has counselled me to go to Mistress Dorothy, and just to tell her all my story.'

'Oh, I am so glad!' I said, jumping up, 'so very glad.'

'Hush, hush, Willie; do not fancy that I have any hope. I know quite well how it must be. But perhaps Janet is right, and that the time has come when it is better that she should hear it. It may be, too, that in her loneliness the knowledge of a love as true, as strong, and faithful as I know mine is for her, will be a comfort to her.'

We went to Morechester, my master saying, when we started, 'Willie, we will not talk, if you please.'

Perhaps all that long silent journey he was getting ready the speech he meant to make to Mistress Dorothy. My thoughts, I know, had time to wander very far afield.

They say that distance makes things look more beautiful. Alas! it also makes them seem far easier. Before we got near Morechester Master Caleb's composure was all gone. His resolution, doggedly held to, he had kept safe, but the morning's calmness, eloquence and steadiness were all lost by the way.

We had settled that I was to wait in the poor Professor's study while he spoke to Mistress Dorothy in the parlour.

I had scarcely been in the room since that day, that seemed so long ago, when Professor Bruce was beginning to pack up his books, and Mistress Dorothy laughed at him for making the room untidy. It was not untidy now. All was in dreary order, speaking sadly in its cold lifelessness of the master that would never return to it.

No one was in the parlour, and Master Caleb came back to the study, walking on tiptoe and speaking almost in a whisper.

'I have sent to ask if she will see me,' he said; 'I expect that she will send for me immediately. You wait here, Willy: that's all you have to do. Just stay quietly where you are.'

He was pushing me backwards all the time, without very well knowing what he was about. At last he got me into the window, and told me again to wait there for him.

'It won't take long,' he said, turning a shade greyer than before, 'and then'——

The door opened, and Mistress Dorothy herself came into the room. She moved so quietly that Master Caleb, staring out of window at the blank wall, clasping and unclasping his hands nervously, did not hear or see her until she spoke his name.

He turned round with a great start and went to meet her.

'Mistress Dorothy, I hope you will forgive me for coming so soon. I just happened to be passing, and so'——

Happened to be passing! In my corner I could not help wondering at Master Caleb. But it was very uncomfortable not to be able to get out—I was hidden by the window-curtain, Mistress Dorothy had not seen me, and my master, I was quite sure, had forgotten all about me. They stood just in the way of the door, and I knew that if I disturbed Master Caleb now, he would never be able to begin speaking to Mistress Dorothy again. There was nothing for it but to read a book, and try not to listen, but my heart was beating fast. I could not help hearing.

Dorothy held out her hand with her frank smile. 'I have been wishing to see you, to thank you for your great goodness to my father and to me,' she said. 'It was kind of you to come.'

'It was Janet—my sister—sent me. She said I ought to come now. I should never have thought of such a thing if it had not been for her.'

'I am glad you came,' she answered. She looked very white and small in her black gown, and her face was grave and sad. The steady straightforward look and smile, however, were not the least changed.

She pushed a chair towards Master Caleb, but he did not seem to see it, and she remained standing too.

'Mistress Dorothy,' he began again, clearing his throat vehemently, 'dear Mistress Dorothy, forgive me for asking you—what are you going to do?'

She hesitated a little, and then said quietly, 'I do not quite know yet. I have been thinking about it, but as yet I have not made up my mind.'

'I thought perhaps I might ask,' went on Master Caleb, 'because'—he made a short stop here, and I heard my own heart beating—'because you know you are your father's daughter.'

She smiled then—smiled and sighed too.

'You are always very kind to me,' she said. 'When I have thought of what I had better do, I shall like to tell you, and I know that you will help me.'

'There's but little I can do,' he said bluntly, and then came another silence. He was gathering together all his strength, and she stood waiting for him to speak.

I scarcely think she caught his meaning directly when he did.

'I could never have said this, if things had been different,' were his words. 'I should never have thought of it. You must forgive me now. It is only because you have no better home. Oh, Mistress Dorothy, I know it is not good enough to ask you to; but would you—could you come to my home?'

The colour rushed into her face. I saw her put out her hand quickly, as if she wanted something to hold by. She made some exclamation, too low for me to hear.

'If I could serve you,' he went on, 'without asking such a great thing as this, believe me I would not trouble you, but I could see no other way. I could not help naming it to you. If there were some brighter life before you, and I could be sure that you were happy, I think I should be satisfied; but now you are alone, and I cannot bear to think of it.'

The tears were in her eyes. Once more she held out her hand towards him, and, grasping his, she spoke very softly. 'Dear friend, it is so good of you—so very good, but——'

'Hush,' he answered quickly, drawing back. 'Yes, I know, I understand. I always knew it must be so, forgive me.'

'Forgive you! the truest, the only friend I have.'

'It was just that. If some one, with a better right than mine, had claimed the great happiness of taking care of you, I would have said no word; but I thought—that is, Janet thought—we might venture just to say how welcome—how proud—how glad——'

'I know how faithful you are. I know you are sorry for me, but you must not——'

'I will not. I never will again. Let me be your friend, Dorothy, still. Another day I will come back,' he said, trying to smile; 'and you will tell your father's old friend your plans. Let me go now.'

He was gone. She called his name. Surely if he had heard her voice then, he would have come back. I think too, that those last half-choking words of his, first made her understand that he did not come to her because he had been her father's friend, but because he loved her.

I heard the door slammed after Master Caleb. As soon as I could get out without being seen, I ran after him. It was difficult to catch him up, at the pace he walked.

When I reached him, out of breath, he put his hand heavily on my shoulder.

'Master Caleb,' I said, looking up into his face, 'may I speak to you?'

'Not now,' he answered, very gently. 'Not now, my boy. It has all ended, Willie, as I knew it must.'

'I am sorry,' I said boldly; 'but I heard all you and Mistress Dorothy said. I was in the study window, where you put me, sir, and I could not help it.'

He did not heed me much.

'We will not speak of it again, Willie. She was quite right to say no.'

61

'But, Master Caleb, I thought she was going to say "yes."'

He stopped in the road and stared at me.

'Going to say yes!' he repeated slowly.

'Only you would not let her, sir. You gave her no time, and then you went away.'

He still looked hard at me, and shook his head slowly. 'You know very little about it, Willie.'

We walked on a long way in silence. At last he said again, 'You thought she would have said yes?'

'I thought so, sir.'

'You know nothing at all about it.'

When we reached home there was Mrs. Janet watching eagerly for us. I guessed how much Master Caleb dreaded having to meet and tell her all.

But she only just looked once at him. She asked no questions, she did not even pity him. Only her sudden change of face—the look of concern—the quick sigh of disappointment that she checked instantly—the grave silence that so respected his great sorrow, went to Master Caleb's heart.

I saw him go up to her, kneel down beside her, look up at her, and then—no, I must have been mistaken—grown-up men like Master Caleb never cry.

School had scarcely begun the next morning when I was mysteriously called out by Mrs. Janet, and found her arrayed in the best bonnet and gown, that usually never saw the light except on Sundays.

'William Lisle,' she began sternly, 'I have been thinking over things. They cannot go on as they are now. They must not be suffered to go on.'

I said, 'No, ma'am,' and waited wondering.

'Something must be done,' pursued Mrs. Janet, in the same severe tone. 'It must be seen to, and that immediately. It passes my understanding how the girl can have behaved to Caleb Morton as she did.'

I was so confounded at hearing Mistress Dorothy—our Mistress Dorothy—Master Caleb's star, spoken of as 'the girl,' that I stared at Mrs. Janet and could say nothing.

'She must have been out of her senses, I verily believe; I can make no other excuse for her. She must have been out of her senses when she said no to such a one as Caleb.'

'I don't think she meant to say it,' I said, in a low voice, feeling as if I myself had been found guilty of refusing to marry Master Caleb.

62

'You don't think that she meant it? Very well. Then why did she say it? Answer me that, William Lisle. Why did she say what she did not mean? It's that question I mean to have an answer to, though I go to Morechester myself to get it.'

'To Morechester! you?' I said. 'Does Master Caleb know?'

'Do as you are bid, Willie, and don't put foolish questions. I don't ask you to give me your advice, but to run across to Furzy Nook and borrow Farmer Foster's gig directly. Bring it up to where the four roads meet, and I will get in there. One would say you were Lord Mayor of London, Willie, you are so ready to put in your word.'

An hour afterwards I received her parting instructions not to leave Master Caleb till she came home again, and only to tell him that she had gone out on some business of her own.

'And I am sure that's the truth. It is my business to reason with the girl,' murmured Mrs. Janet to herself, as she clambered up to her high seat with a struggle; 'she's got neither father nor mother, and a good bit of plain speaking does nobody any harm.'

'Gee up, Dobbin,' said Farmer Foster, shaking the horse's reins, and the next moment I stood at the cross roads, looking with wondering eyes after Mrs. Janet, who, driven by Farmer Foster himself, was disappearing in the high-backed gig round the well-known corner of the road to Morechester.

All the day I felt guilty whenever I met Master Caleb's eye, thinking that he would insist on knowing whither his sister had betaken herself in so unwonted a way. But he was quite satisfied with my first confused sentence about business, and Farmer Foster, and in truth seemed to have little heart for inquiring after anybody.

Afternoon came, but without bringing Mrs. Janet. Evening drew on, school broke up, and Master Caleb, who had kept hard at work all day, sat down with his head leaning on his hands, and gave himself up unresistingly to his sad thoughts.

At last, after I had stood for full an hour leaning over the garden gate, listening eagerly, but in vain, for the sound of wheels, one of the farm boys from Farmer Foster's came sauntering—taking his time about it too—over the stile and along the lane from Furzy Nook.

Mrs. Janet was there, and had sent for me. Conscious of being mixed up in a plot, and standing in wholesome awe of Mrs. Janet, I was dismayed when Master Caleb got up wearily, saying that if Janet was at the Farm he supposed he might as well go and fetch her home. Would not the secret of Mrs. Janet's journey come out somehow, if Master Caleb went with me? and then whatever was to become of me? Much troubled in mind, but quite unable to stop him, I followed his footsteps across the fields.

The sun was setting over Furzy Nook, reddening the old house and making its many lattice windows shine like gold.

Dame Foster met us at her garden gate, her apron, as of old, quite full of flowers. 'You are kindly welcome, Master Caleb,' she said; 'yes, your good sister is here; will you go in and speak to her?'

I ran on in front. 'Mrs. Janet,' I began, pushing open the parlour door in a great hurry, 'Master Caleb is come too, and——'

I stopped short, for there stood Dorothy.

Master Caleb was close behind me, and at this moment, just when it was most needed, Mrs. Janet completely lost all presence of mind.

She tried to put herself before Dorothy, to hide her, but Master Caleb had already seen her, and stood at the door as if he were turned into stone.

There was a dreadful long minute, and then Dorothy came slowly forward. She had a colour in her cheeks that I had never seen before, but she spoke almost as quietly as ever—

'Master Caleb, Mrs. Janet brought me here.'

'Janet! and you let her—you came?'

'I came,' she said, the red flush deepening in her cheeks, 'because you asked me yesterday.'

'Did Janet say I was unhappy?'

'She said,'—he bent down, for he could scarcely catch the words—'she said you really wanted me.'

Master Caleb grasped both her hands.

'Dorothy, did you come to me because you pitied me?'

'No, Master Caleb,' she said simply, 'because I was glad to come.'

It was not the words only, but something in her voice, that made him say suddenly, 'Oh Dorothy! oh Dorothy!'

Until that moment we had quite forgotten, Mrs. Janet and I, that we ought not to be there. But now, as he bent his head down lower and lower over the clasped hands he held, Mrs. Janet with a sudden pull drew me out into the passage, and shut the door upon them.

'Bless their foolish hearts, poor dears,' she ejaculated drying her eyes vehemently in the passage.

'Oh Mrs. Janet,' I could not help saying, in the fulness of my heart, 'how glad I am that it has come right.'

'Come right!' she echoed, turning round on me.

'Come right! of course it has, Willie Lisle. Who ever thought it wouldn't? There were no two ways about it.'

* * * *

Master Caleb and Dorothy were married from Furzy Nook.

A wedding was of all things in the world the most delightful to Farmer Foster and his wife. A few hours only were needed to make them take Mistress Dorothy home to their hearts as if she had been a grandchild of their own. The sweet quiet face, the black gown, and the little touch of romance in the story of her presence there, won their own welcome.

Every one was soon persuaded, very willingly, that it would be simple madness for Dorothy to go back alone to the sad house at Morechester.

'We couldn't think for an instant of suffering such a thing, Mrs. Janet, neither I, nor yet my master; and then, Furzy Nook will be so handy, "somebody" can get to see her every day!' and the old dame nodded slyly to Master Caleb, who did not see her, and then looked across kindly at the farmer, remembering how he used to come a-courting in the summer evenings, so many, many years ago.

The troth plight had scarcely been given and received—the engaged pair had but half begun to realise that they were to belong to each other some day, before Dame Foster had mentally frosted over the huge wedding-cake, and doomed to death the fat capons that were to grace the marriage feast.

It was a proud day on which Master Caleb brought his betrothed to see the Castle. He whispered to me that he had waited for a fine day. Truly he had chosen happily. The ruins were all a-glow with burning sunlight. Our grey towers looked set in warmth and colour. Orange wall-flower, tufts of scarlet poppies, feathery silver grasses, golden dandelions, had forced their way through crevices in the old walls; downy thistles shone with their purple blossoms, crimson woodbine went climbing where it would. Covering all grew the many-hued mosses and lichens, russet and grey, golden, red and brown.

Glittering light here and there; violet shadows; brilliant butterflies hovering over the clover tufts; the warm fragrance of wild thyme; a few sheep cropping the short grass, one of them carrying a bell that tinkled lazily and pleasantly as he moved.

Yes, it was a good day for Mistress Dorothy, to see it all. Master Caleb took her round very slowly, stopping often. We saw him pointing and explaining, drawing lines in the air with a stick, to show where broken fragments of stone told of fallen buildings and grass-

65

grown banquetting halls.

'Poor thing!' said Cuthbert, as we stood watching them from the mound.

'Why poor thing?' I asked indignantly.

'He's teaching her,' Cuthbert said, in a melancholy voice; 'I suppose he's always at it.'

'I tell you she likes it.'

Cuthbert looked at me, and began to whistle—that clear birdlike whistle of his, that no one could help listening to. I saw Mistress Dorothy turn round and look up towards him with a smile.

'Over the hills and far away,' he whistled gaily, and the birds sang the chorus, and the sun shone. Master Caleb and Dorothy went rambling in and out through shade and sunshine. I could not help thinking what a pleasant thing life was.

And next came the wedding day.

It was to be a very quiet one, because the little bride was still grieving for the kind old father who was not there to give her his blessing. So everybody kept on repeating that it must be quite quiet. That is to say, no one was to go to the church who could by any possibility be persuaded to stay away. But unluckily nobody could be so persuaded. Master Caleb belonged to all of us. No one—certainly not Dorothy—would have wished that the scholars, who had suddenly found out how fond they were of him, should not go to his wedding. They forgave him on that day all his strange love for three-syllabled words, and sums in Long Division. They forgot how hardly he had often used them in respect to learning things by heart, and only strove who could shout himself the most hoarse in his honour.

All the village was waiting round the porch long before the wedding party came out of church. How the sun shone that morning! What merry peals the bells sent out upon the golden air! How cheer after cheer rang forth, as Master Caleb, in such a coat, such black silk stockings, such shoe-buckles as Wyncliffe had never before dreamt of, came out bareheaded into the sunshine, from the deep shade of the porch, and led his bride by the hand all through the shouting crowd! The village girls, with Hildred at their head, showered baskets-full of red roses before Mistress Dorothy as she walked!

Master Caleb could get out nothing but 'I thank you, friends, I thank you;' and Dorothy held out both hands, right and left, to meet the eager ones stretched out to greet her.

Then we young ones climbed up trees and stood on the top of walls to give them one cheer more, as they drove off to Furzy Nook, and the old folk called down blessings on the sweet face that was bright with smiles and tears.

Another cheer when the bride, God bless her, waved her handkerchief to us just before they turned the corner. Another, when Farmer Foster bade all there come down to Furzy Nook to drink her health. Yet one more, a hearty one, for Mrs. Janet, arm-in-arm with the farmer; and then, again and again, for the old schoolhouse and its master. Thus we welcomed Mistress Morton home to Wyncliffe.

> *O little feet! that such long years*
> *Must wander on through hopes and fears—*
> *Must ache and bleed beneath your load;*
> *I, nearer to the wayside inn,*
> *Where toil shall cease and rest begin,*
> *Am weary thinking of your road!*

LONGFELLOW.

* * * *

Wandering Willie paused. The clock struck. The outer door of the farm-house kitchen opened. A gust of snowy wind rushed in, and the farmer followed, after stopping to shake the snow from his hat, and to stamp it off his long boots in the porch.

Another door opened too. In came 'mother,' proclaiming bedtime.

There was a general petition to be allowed to stay up a little longer.

'Only till the end of the story,' the children begged.

'For it's just done, mother,' said little Cecily, who had been fast asleep on the old man's shoulder for nearly an hour past. 'It's just done;' and her blue eyes tried in vain to keep wide open.

'Oh Cecily,' called the rest of the children indignantly, 'it isn't nearly done. And you've been asleep all the time. We big ones may stay, mother?'

But mother shook her head.

Then one of the little sisters said she did not so much mind going to bed, because nearly everybody in the story was grown up now, and stories about grown-up people were very dull. So she took Cecily's hand, and the two little maidens ran off together, laughing.

'It's as wild a night as ever I saw,' said the farmer, standing before the blazing fire. 'There'll be no getting across the moor to-morrow, Willie. You'll just have to be content and bide here.'

'And we shall hear the end of the story to-morrow evening,' said Lois.

When to-morrow evening came, the same group had gathered round the hearth. Again bed-time came round, and the little ones dropped off one by one, until only Lois and Roger were left to listen. But whenever the old man paused they said 'Go on, go on.' And he went on, drawn by their listening faces. By-and-by the mother came and joined them when she had seen that the children were warm and safe in bed,—all the merry eyes closed and the restless limbs at rest.

She came and listened too, to hear what it was that had so moved her pretty Lois, that the tears were in her eyes; both she and Roger were holding Willie's hands and looking with kindly pity into the old man's face.

But the busy wife and mother, full of life's joys and cares, could see nothing to cry about in a story of what had come and gone so many years ago.

Only she listened patiently to the end, because she too loved Wandering Willie.

PART II.

A great oak in Wyncliffe Chase was doomed to be cut down.

It was a goodly, wide-spreading tree, too wide-spreading indeed, for some of its branches came in the way of a certain forest-king, a huge-limbed mighty giant among trees, within whose stately area of space no neighbour was allowed to trespass. So the younger tree was to come down.

It met its fate on a sparkling autumn day. There was just a touch of sharpness in the air. The woods were mostly green still, though already plenty of red and brown and yellow patches told that autumn was upon us. The horse-chestnuts shining on the ground near their empty white shells, and the crimson and purple leaves of the bramble-bushes belonged to autumn too.

Now it is the old story. I have forgotten the great things and remembered the small. Nine years or more had passed since Caleb Morton's marriage. We had been growing up all this time, and changing by little and little, outwardly and inwardly. We left school and set about our business in life—Cuthbert became second forester under Clifford, Hildred's brother, and I had lately begun to be old Farmer Foster's bailiff at Furzy Nook.

How all these changes came about by degrees I have well-nigh forgotten. But I remember quite well the pheasants crowing in the wood that day, and the dead gold fern, and the voices that talked and laughed round the falling tree.

And out of the mists of failing memory, where they have been hidden for so long, Cuthbert and Hildred, and I myself, seem to come forth again distinctly on that autumn morning; Cuthbert and I no longer boys, Hildred a girl, not any more a child.

Cuthbert raised his axe, and struck and struck, until he was fain, for want of breath, to draw back, and turn towards us and laugh. Hildred sat on the trunk of a fallen tree, with a great bundle of sticks she had been gathering, tied up in a red handkerchief at her feet, and I stood near her—sometimes speaking to her, oftener full of thoughts that were an idle many-coloured medley, brightly-tinted as the autumn woods themselves.

First of all it was sweet, passing sweet, to stand there beside Hildred. That was an old thought. It remained the same, while the rest shifted, and flitted to and fro, first one way, then another, like leaves that the wind plays with and blows about as it will. The tree—it would not be standing half an hour hence. Where would the rooks that had built in it for three summers past have their nest next spring? Cuthbert's strokes bit deeper into the tough heart-of-oak than any of the others. He was stronger even than Matt Clifford. Poor tree, it was hard for it, Hildred said just now, to leave its fair woodland world. Yes, and it would be hard to leave a great many things if one had to do so, first and foremost—I broke off there, for they had got a rope round the trunk, and Clifford called out to the men to stand clear. The great tree tottered. Hildred shouted with the rest, and clapped her hands.

Well, I must see it down now, though I really ought to be where the ploughs are going over the sunny 'Seven Acres,' on the hill, a mile away from here. Then I looked again at Hildred, perched laughing on her mossy seat, with the golden fern at her feet and the dark woods behind her, and I tried to find a rhyme to the word 'winsome' to end some verses I had been making in my head.

Master Caleb Morton had not given up lending me books, in the years since I had ceased to be a scholar of his, and ploughmen and shepherds, he told me, had been poets before now; so I tried to make verses too. I kept them very secret, never telling anyone about them, not even Hildred—whom indeed they chiefly concerned—or Cuthbert. Many an hour's hard work I beguiled by stringing my rhymes together, always hoping I was making something that would be beautiful.

But I was a poor scholar, for all Cuthbert and Hildred said, I was fonder of hard words than Master Caleb himself. My lines would not often come right. I was not good at putting my thoughts in harness. They were like a team that will not go together. Some got on too fast and covered too much ground, and others stood still, or else wanted to go off at quite a different pace. So I got disheartened. Besides, what was the use of such poor words as I could find? If I called the sunshine 'golden,' was that half bright enough for the life-giving light? And if I said the wind whispered, or the river sang, it was not what I meant.

Sometimes at night I thought I had made something very good, and went to sleep contented, but in the morning, when I said over my verses, all the meaning seemed to have gone out of them. I said to myself at last, 'You are very weak, and Nature is very strong. She can speak to your heart and tell you all things; but it is not given you to repeat what she says to others. From henceforth listen, but in silence.' And so I gave up making verses. I have listened all my life long, and now that I am old, I try once more to say a little of what I have been hearing all these years. And perhaps because I am more humble and expect less, perhaps because my eye and ear are growing duller, I am not so discontented as I once was. I know my words are poor, but I am waiting. Soon I shall learn the new song that they sing up there, beyond the sunlight, and then I shall be satisfied.

However, I had not got to that yet. I went on trying to find my rhyme, and failed, as better people may have done before me.

It was a pity. The word winsome might have been made for Hildred. Mistress Dorothy Morton, years ago, had called her the picture of a child. I am sure she was the picture of a maiden now. It was a very fair flower that had bloomed in our grey old ruin.

Those bygone times, when we used to let Hildred go about with us now and then, as a great treat for her, were very wonderful to look back to. Now I prized every minute that she lighted up with her sunbeam pleasure.

The knowledge of what she was to me, had come so gradually that I cannot remember when I first felt that my life-choice was made, and that the world held for me but one thing worth living for. I had been sure of it for many a long day, before I dreamed of putting the love I bore her into words. Nearly all my life it must have lain deep down in my heart, like a seed that, buried in the ground, waits for the coming of the spring; and now, in the spring and sunshine of my young manhood, it had risen up in blossom and in fruit.

'Willie, here comes your father,' said Hildred presently, jumping up and running off to meet him. They liked each other, those two. My father—it was no wonder certainly—had smiles and even words for her, such as he was never known to bestow on anyone else. Hildred was not a bit afraid of him, though other people said he became more 'dour' and hard as he got on in life. She came along by his side now, suiting her light footsteps to his heavy tread; he nodded now and then in answer to her merry chatter, and a look of slow contentment stole over his face. She made him stop for a moment to watch the wood-cutters, and as they stood looking on, the tree came crashing down at last.

Our idling time was over as soon as my father came. I turned away, and Hildred raised the bundle of sticks on to her head, and moved towards home.

'I haven't been losing much time,' she said, looking up at him merrily from under its shadow. 'Look, all these for Granny.'

'Good girl,' he answered, and he even stood still to watch her carrying it lightly in and out among the trees, and singing as she went.

Hildred never let the grass grow under her feet. She was always up and about. The bundle of sticks that pleased my father was only of a piece with all her sunny, helpful ways. She had gathered sticks for Granny hundreds of times before, only it was fated that this bundle should first put a thought into my father's head that he pondered over in his slow way all through the winter.

He told it to me one evening in the early spring, as we were going home from work together. I saw him looking round at me once or twice, as if there was something he had a mind to say, if he had known how to set about it.

'Grandmother's got to be an old woman,' he began at last, but after I had said 'yes,' he did not appear for some time to have anything to add.

'We need some one younger to keep the house,' he went on presently. 'I say, Will, do you ever think anything about getting married?'

I certainly did think of it very often indeed—a good deal oftener than I cared to tell my father. The question took me so by surprise that I scarcely knew how to answer it. At last I said bashfully, that 'perhaps I might, odd times.'

'Ha! 'cause if so be she's a stirring, thrifty lass, I don't care how soon you do.'

'If I could, I don't know if Hildred would,' I stammered, more astonished than ever, for I had always thought that I should have to make a home of my own, before I could ask Hildred to marry me.

My father nodded gravely once or twice when he heard her name. 'I thought as much,' he muttered, more to himself than to me, 'She'll do.' And as we reached home he stopped to say, 'Then you can bring your wife home here whensoever it suits yourself. I'm agreeable, lad, without any more waste of words.'

Without any more words with him, but a great many with myself. My wife—Hildred! That soft, sparkling little creature, that no trouble ought to come near—such was my thought then—or sorrow touch. Would she let me try to take care of her? Would she come to the grey old gate-house some day in her butterfly brightness and beauty, and fold her wings there, and be my own? Little Hildred, whom my mother used to love and pet in the old days. It seemed strange that we were longing for her now to fill my mother's place. But would she come?

That was the one question. I wearied myself with finding answers to it. Hildred herself, I was sure, little knew all that she was to me. No one had found it out, I believed, except my father, with that odd silent watchfulness of his. Not even Cuthbert—I almost wished he had, that I might have talked to him about it; but he never guessed my one secret, and somehow I could not make up my mind to tell him.

No, I must ask Hildred herself first; and now there would be many long days to live through before I even saw her again. For on the morrow I had to go away to see my dear old master, Caleb Morton, and it might be a fortnight before I could get back to Wyncliffe. Granny and Cuthbert and Matt Clifford were all standing round when I said good-bye to Hildred. It was a great pity that my father had waited to speak, until my last day at home. I had been reckoning on my journey beforehand, but now I should only count the days until I could come back.

It was two years since I had seen Master Caleb. A very dark day it had been for Wyncliffe when he gave up the school, and went to be master to a much larger one a long way off. But it was such a piece of good fortune as he had long deserved, and his friends could only rejoice for him even while they mourned over losing him.

His new home was in a busy sea-port town, as different as possible from quiet Wyncliffe. Instead of trees, they had the crowded masts of the shipping in the harbour to look at. Huge bales of merchandise piled up along the quays; sailors of all countries and tongues thronging the streets and waterside; vessels continually gliding into port or gliding out again on their paths over the sea. This, in exchange for the harvest fields and the blue hills at home. The smell of salt and tar on the sea-breeze, instead of the breath of flowering lime-trees. And the queer-sounding languages shouted by foreign voices, were very different from the distant cries of field labourers, and the cawing of the rooks, round Wyncliffe schoolhouse. Only, to make up for all, there was the solemn beauty and wonder of the sea.

Words cannot utter it, or, once seen, memory lose hold of its vastness.

It mattered little to Master Caleb and his wife where their lot was cast. They carried their own sunshine with them, and would have been happy anywhere; still, they were faithful in heart to their first home, and had been longing, Mistress Morton told me, for the sight of a Wyncliffe face.

I was to have stayed with them for ten days. I was three months away from home. On what was to have been the last day of my stay, Master Caleb and I were overtaken in a thunder-storm, as we were driving home from a distance along the coast. I never quite knew how it happened. The horse took fright at the lightning. It was a dark evening, and Master Caleb, not much skilled in driving, had the reins. We went over the rocks together, horse and gig and all. Master Caleb escaped, fortunately, with a few bruises, and I broke my leg.

It might have been much worse. I was taken home to Master Caleb's house, and Mrs. Janet nursed me. Those weary weeks that I lay unable to move, would not have seemed so endless if it had not been for my longing to get home to Hildred. But for that, I should have been well content. After the first days of racking pain were over, and I came back to the knowledge of outward things, I used to lie and watch the little scenes of household life that passed like pictures before my eyes, and think how pleasantly true to my remembrance of them my old friends were. Master Caleb, creeping up to my bedside laden with books, in the full security that even at the worst they must be the best cure for pain or fever—Mrs. Janet, ordering him and them scornfully away, coming in with her business step and skilful hand, the very model of a sick-nurse; prompt of action, short, positive, and encouraging of speech. How like their old selves they were! And Mistress Dorothy, just to have her there to look at, did me more good than anything else. None of the power of comfort or healing had gone from her voice and smile. To her only I could talk of Hildred. Of course I had told her all about that. She only could quiet the restlessness that grew on me as the slow days dragged on.

It seemed so hard to be away just then from Hildred. How was I to keep still, thinking of what might have been by this time, if I had been able to go home. Never before had I been without seeing her for so long. I dreamt of her whenever I fell asleep, always the same dream, that she was in trouble, and I could not move to help her.

Cuthbert, too, that was another trouble; how was he getting on with my father all this time? When I was at home I could generally keep things pretty straight between them, but they did not understand each other. My father never cared for him; the little he said to him was sharp and harsh. And Cuthbert—what wonder?—could not always bear it well. He had a high spirit, and for all his sweet temper, he liked to take his own way, and, once taken, chose to keep it. If I could only hope that he would be patient now, or that my father would not try him with some of those sharp bitter words that stung so deeply!

It was no use Mrs. Janet's telling me that an easy mind helped to mend broken bones. It might be so, but an easy mind was quite beyond my reach.

Dorothy did better than preach patience, she shared my impatience. As often as I pleased she was ready to count over with me the weary days that they said must pass before I was fit for a journey. Also she charmed long hours away by letting me talk of Hildred.

My release came at last. I could walk pretty stoutly with a stick, by the time that the coach dropped me, just after dusk on an evening in June, at the crossing of the four roads, close to Wyncliffe village.

Before I got into the straggling little street, I heard music in front of me—fifes and drums sounding noisily through the quiet of the summer's evening. It was a recruiting party—no unusual sight in those war days. As I overtook them I was told that I was a fine fellow, and asked if I would not join them and fight for the King.

They were just going into the Castle—the public-house—when I passed, and as I turned my head to look at the light that was streaming from it, I heard my own name called suddenly. The next moment Cuthbert came out and joined me.

'Willie! thank Heaven you are come. Are you better?' he said, seizing my hand and wringing it.

'Yes. What's the matter, Cuthbert? what are you doing here?'

He did not answer, but moved so as to stand in the circle of light from the open door. I looked at him again, and saw the gay ribands that the recruits wear, fluttering from his hat.

'Cuthbert!'

'Yes, you see I have enlisted. Why, Will, I did not think you would mind it so much;' for, thunderstruck I leant against the wall to gather breath. He put his hand on my shoulder.

'It's not worth troubling about.'

'You can be bought off,' I said, recovering myself.

'Not for the world. Why should I? I did it of my own free will, for I can't stay here, and I won't.'

'Why, what has come to you?'

He was very pale, I saw, and his hands shook. He looked as if some great storm of trouble or anger had passed over him. After a minute's pause he said suddenly, 'Did you know that your father kept a store of money, gold guineas, and shillings, and a five-pound note, in an old teapot in the cupboard behind his bed?'

'What are you talking about? No.'

'No more did I,' said Cuthbert. 'Well, he lost it.'

'But what has that to do with you?'

Cuthbert gave an odd short laugh. 'Only that he says I took it.'

'I don't understand.'

'Perhaps you think so too,' he said bitterly. 'No, Will, you know I did not mean that, but they've driven me half out of my senses with all this.'

'Cuthbert, my father never said you had taken his money.'

'Said it, or thought it, it pretty nearly comes to the same thing. I understood well enough what he was after, so I'm off. Never mind that now. We can't talk here, and I've got something to say to you. We don't go until to-morrow morning, so I can walk back with you.'

'You're coming home for to-night, at all events?'

'I can't go there,' said Cuthbert his lip trembling, 'not to your father's house. Clifford will take me in.'

He turned and spoke to some one inside the house. There was a confused noise of singing and loud laughter, and the jingling of glasses from the bar. In a minute Cuthbert came out again, and said it was all right. He need not be there until sunrise the next day.

'Come on,' he said impatiently, and he began to walk up the street with long, quick strides.

'Now tell me,' I said.

Cuthbert's mood had changed. 'There's little enough to tell,' he answered quietly, 'only that I've enlisted. After all, I'm a soldier's son, and I know the life. I've always had a hankering after it, as you know.'

'But my father, what has he done? Try and tell me.'

'It's all along of this money. He's been scraping it and hoarding it together for ever so long. He thought no one knew about it. No more they did. But two days ago he missed it.'

Cuthbert had begun quietly, but now his eyes were lighting again, and his voice quickened. 'And he thinks I took it. *I* to take his money! and your father, too.'

'He couldn't think so. You must have made some great mistake.'

'Not I. I saw what he was at well enough. Don't you think I know he's always hated me? You know it too, Will, though you've tried so hard to keep me from finding it out. He was mad when he found his money gone, and he spoke out then pretty plain—as he never did before.'

'He didn't say you took it.'

'Not at first—not straight out, till I asked him what he meant—he did then. I wouldn't stay another day after that. You wouldn't have had me stay, Will?'

'There were others there,' he went on again, 'when he accused me of knowing more of the money than I cared to say. Hildred was there.'

'She didn't believe it of you.'

'God bless her, no.'

I put my hand on his arm. 'Cuthbert, you ought to stay here, don't you see?'

He looked at me.

'You mean they'll say I've gone off with the money. No, they won't say that. I thought I'd told you the money was found again.'

'Found!'

'Yes, but that made no odds. I can't stay where I've been served as your father served me.'

'But who found it?'

'The money? Oh, it was all Granny's doing.' Cuthbert smiled. 'Poor Granny, she had taken the teapot away, not knowing.'

'What did father say?'

'I don't know. I didn't stay to hear. I tell you it was all one, after what he had thought of me. Will, I, that he took in—though that was your doing and your mother's, not his. I, that had grown up in his house and thought I was like his son. I wish he had turned me out of doors when your mother died. Maybe some day I may feel as grateful to him for his charity as I ought to be. I can't now.

'I did not mean to say aught of this to you, old chap,' he went on sadly. 'I ought not, only I can't help it. It wouldn't any of it have happened if you had been at home.'

'Then let me get you off,' I said eagerly. 'Let me do something for you.'

'Yes, that you shall, but not that. What a mercy it is that you have got home in time! It wasn't all this I wanted to tell you about. I was going to write you a letter, but talking is much handier.'

'And you must go?'

'Yes.' He took a shilling out of his pocket and held it up in the dim light with a half-laugh. 'Never mind that; it's done. Will, what I wanted to say to you besides good-bye was this.' His voice had grown grave enough now. 'I have something to leave in your charge.'

I don't know why my heart stopped beating for a second, and then went on again quicker than before.

'Do you know what it is?' Cuthbert continued. 'The greatest treasure I have—the only thing in all the world that really belongs to me.'

'What?' I asked.

And he answered, 'Hildred.'

We had left the village behind by this time. We were on the bit of road before you reach the bridge, and the Castle was in front of us. Often in the evening, when the twilight has gathered, and the air is heavy with dew, and with a faint sweet smell of newly cut hay, I live that moment over again. I see Cuthbert's face turned towards me, pale and eager, in the half-darkness. I see the white road, and the moon just rising solemn and fiery red over the Castle. I feel the silence, except that the familiar rush of falling water, unheard for months, was beginning to sound in my ears again.

I never crossed the bridge afterwards, by night or day, and came within ear-shot of the waterfall, without hearing Cuthbert's voice say 'Hildred.'

For the next few minutes I don't know what he said. The dusty road—I noticed even then how dusty it was—seemed to rise up before my face. I put out my hand to hold by Cuthbert's arm. He thought that, being still lame, I was tired, and meant to lean on him, and he drew my arm over his shoulder, supporting me as we climbed up the grassy hill that was the short cut to the ruins. Presently I knew that he was saying—'It is hard for her.'

'Does Hildred know you have enlisted?'

'Yes, yes, poor child. I told her, and then, when it was too late, I found out how much I loved her.'

'Does she care for you?'

'Yes,' he answered very softly. 'Yes indeed, thank God.'

'But oh, Willie, you will take care of her for me. Don't let her forget me. I trust her to you entirely. Promise me you will be good to her. Watch over her for me.'

The tears were in his eyes. He was going away. It might be that I should never see him again. This was no time to think of my shattered hopes, my ruined life.

'If I could do any good,' I began to say. He interrupted me. 'You can—you can. It is everything to me. Let me think she has somebody near her who will be kind to her—who will comfort her if she is unhappy—who will never let them make her give me up.'

'She will not do that if she cares.'

'No, but I can't help fearing. Tell her how I love her. Talk to her about me. Promise me.' And he held out his hand.

I took it. I felt what a hard promise it was that he called on me to make—how little he guessed what he was asking of me. I knew how much it would cost me to keep it. A dread came over me like a shadow of the trouble that was to come through this.

But I would not listen. Cuthbert loved her, and she—yes, she loved him. He was going away, and he trusted me.

I only said two words, and then I had pledged myself, and shut the door on the long hope of years.

We were within the walls now. Cuthbert, with a few fervent words of thanks, turned towards Clifford's house, and I went home.

Granny gave a little cry of joy when I opened the kitchen door.

'My dear,' she said, hardly waiting to greet me, 'the very thing I have been wishing for, is for you to come home. We're in sad trouble, Willie. Do you know where Cuthbert is?'

'He came back with me just now.'

'I'm thankful for that. One couldn't tell what the poor boy might do. Willie, my dear, he and father had words,' said Granny, coming close and whispering mysteriously. 'It's about the money in the teapot, and it's all my fault.'

'Where's father?' I asked.

'Hush, he's upstairs now, counting It. He's always counting it, I think. That was where it was, you see. He was called away of a sudden when he was just putting something into the teapot, and he left the cupboard door open; and I came in and saw it. It was my old teapot, Willie, and I was glad to see it again, and so——'

'Granny, I want to go and speak to father.'

'So you shall, my dear; but just you wait and hear me first. And so, my dear—what was I going to say? It was my old teapot, and I used to keep odd halfpence in it, and stand it on the mantel-shelf. He took it away. I thought I'd lost it d'ye see, Willie?'

'Yes, Granny, I see. Will you——'

Granny held my arm tighter, and still whispering went on. 'My dear, I'm right vexed. I shouldn't ha' done it, but I meant no harm. When I saw my teapot, I took it thinking it was nobbut my coppers as made it heavy. Stephen missed it, and Cuthbert was there.'

'What did he say to Cuthbert?'

'My dear, they had words. Clifford, he came in, and Hildred. When I got into the room father sat there mazed-like about his money, and Cuthbert was standing as it might be here. I told them, and I brought back the teapot directly, my dear, but it was too late. Cuthbert flung out of the house and——. Hush, Willie, here's father coming downstairs.'

He came in. He looked surprised, and as it seemed to me only half pleased to see me.

'Father,' said my grandmother, 'Cuthbert's got back.'

My father looked up. 'I thought he'd come. What's he been about?'

'He's enlisted,' I said sadly.

I could not tell whether my father was surprised, or glad, or sorry. He said nothing, but I noticed that he gave me one or two quick looks from under his shaggy eyebrows.

'Father,' I said, 'you will see poor Cuthbert before he goes?'

'Humph! I suppose you know he's been beforehand with you with Hildred. Did he tell you that?'

'Yes, he told me. He meant no harm by me. He doesn't know.'

'I wish the lad had never come nigh the place.'

Just as he said this, the door was opened quickly, and Cuthbert came in. He went straight up to my father, the colour coming all over his face, and held out his hand.

'I'm going away to-morrow,' he said, speaking quickly, 'and as like as not I shall never come back again. I am come just to shake hands and thank you before I go, for all you've done for me; I know how much it's been.'

My father was taken by surprise. He put out his hand slowly to meet Cuthbert's.

'About that money,' he began, 'I made a mistake.'

'Thank you,' Cuthbert answered, colouring again. 'I'd sooner you wouldn't say anything of that.'

Still grasping my father's hand, he went on—

'I know I've often vexed you, but you won't be troubled with me any longer, and we part good friends—don't we?' he ended with his frank, sweet smile.

'I'm sure I wish you good luck, lad.'

Cuthbert turned round to me.

It was the one gleam of comfort on that dark night, that those two were at peace together before Cuthbert went away.

The two troubles coming so quick one upon another seemed to have confused me. I wanted time to understand them. Every thought brought a fresh sting, and they kept thronging into my mind, shifting and changing strangely.

Only one thing was clear: I had lost Cuthbert and Hildred both at once. He had gone back to her now, for more last words. I was used to thinking of them as belonging to me. But they belonged to each other now, and I was nothing to them,—not much at least.

Cuthbert was going away to-morrow. A while ago that would have seemed hard enough, but harder still, the Hildred I loved, and who I had thought loved me, was gone already.

Why do I talk about myself? They two who loved each other were the ones to be pitied. To-morrow, when Cuthbert was away, there would be time enough to think.

My father sat by the fire, with his hands and chin resting on his stick, but his eyes followed me whenever I moved. I was not used to being watched like that, and presently I went to the door.

'I say, boy,' he called after me.

I looked round.

'Don't you go and vex yourself. He's going away, and girls soon forget, you know.'

'Girls will be girls, Willie,' said Granny, meaning to be comforting.

I went outside and leaned against the wall. The moon was covered with clouds, and in the hushed darkness you could hear if a leaf stirred or a grasshopper chirped in the long grass.

'Girls soon forget.' Ay, but I had just promised not to let Hildred forget. Besides, she wasn't likely to forget Cuthbert. And did I even wish her to forget him? I did not know. What was the use of thinking?

How long Cuthbert stayed! Granny's flitting light went out upstairs. She, and my father too, were most likely quietly asleep, before I heard his step coming quickly through the darkness.

'You waited for me,' he said, coming up. 'Clifford kept me talking. Come in, will you? I must get my things together. I told you how it would be. Clifford wanted her to take her promise back, because I was going away.'

'She did not?'

He shook his head. 'But I have only you to count on that will help her,' he said sighing.

The packing-up was not a long business, but we went through it very slowly, though we talked little. Who ever said the parting words they had meant to speak at the last? Ours were very few.

Once Cuthbert looked up as he was kneeling on the floor beside the old chest that had held all our goods for so long. 'Will, I can't make speeches, but I am thinking very much to-night of the time you brought me home, and took me for your brother. There never was such a brother. I should like just for once to say, thank you.'

I put my hand on his shoulder and pressed it hard. It was lucky he did not want words, for I had none. We lay down near each other for the last time. I don't know whether Cuthbert cried before he went to sleep. I know I did.

It was soon over the next morning. As we went downstairs in the doubtful light, we could hear my father's heavy breathing. But poor Granny was down before us, with some breakfast ready that no one could eat, and a candle flaring with a sickly ray in the broadening daylight.

'I shall never see thee again, my dear,' Granny said, two slow tears rolling down her face; 'but be a good lad, and don't forget to say thy prayers.'

'I won't, Granny;' and as he kissed her she put her trembling old hand on his brown head and blessed him.

Then Cuthbert went out quickly, and I followed. He stood still for a minute and looked round. He could not have seen the old place look more beautiful than in its morning stillness; the birds were waking up here and there, and a glitter of dew and sunshine lay on the grass.

'Come,' he said, 'it is late.'

Hildred met us under the great yew tree. It had always been a trysting-place of ours, and we used to part there when we were children, coming back from school. Their great parting was to be there now.

He went up to her, and took her in his arms as if he could never leave her. Hildred was crying. She did not say much, but she clung to him and held him fast.

'Dear heart!' he said, kissing her hair softly. 'You must not cry so. Hush, Hildred!'

I did not know how much tenderness there could be in his voice till I heard those broken words—'See, here is our brother Willie. He is going to take care of you for me. He will watch over my dear love when I am gone.'

A few minutes more, and Cuthbert said, 'I must go.'

I did not see their parting. He came to me, grasped both my hands. 'God bless you. Take care of her. Don't let her forget me.'

'I am going with you.'

'No, go back to her. Stay and comfort her. Oh, be good to her, Willie!'

The distant sound of the fifes and drums came from the village down below.

82

'I shall be late.'

Cuthbert was gone. The cliff hid him directly. Those few hours had changed the world for me.

My brother was gone, and I had lost my love.

I went back, as he bade me, to Hildred. She had flung herself down on the ground where he left her, and was crying bitterly. I tried to take her hand and lift her up, but she pushed me away, turning from me and burying her face deeper in her hands.

'Hildred, don't cry like that.'

She shook her head impatiently, and rocked herself backwards and forwards like a child. I did not at all know what to do for her.

'I wish I could comfort you, Hildred.'

'You can't,' she said with a gasping sob.

'No I'm afraid nobody could——'

'Cuthbert could,' she interrupted.

It was the first time I had heard from herself that Cuthbert was more to her than I was, although, of course, I knew it before. The words stung me so much that I felt almost inclined to go away and leave her. But presently she took away her hands and looked up, pushing back the ruffled hair from her forehead. It was such a pitiful little face, her eyes wet and her cheeks crimsoned with tears.

'Oh dear, I am so unhappy,' she said.

I took her hand again.

'Poor little Hildred, I'm very sorry for you.'

'It's all your father's fault,' said Hildred, with a little impatient stamp of her foot upon the ground. 'How could he be so wicked?'

'It was a mistake,' I said, after a moment's pause.

'It was cruel of him. Oh, poor Cuthbert! Why did you let him go?'

'I, Hildred?'

'Yes, how could you? He will just go and be killed in the wars, and then you will be sorry.'

It was weak, almost unmanly, to mind her childish words, but I could not help it. I turned and walked away. The next moment she ran after me.

'Willie, I don't quite mean it; you know I don't.' She looked up with one of her own coaxing smiles. 'Don't be angry; I think being unhappy makes me cross, and I've got such a pain in my throat that I don't know what to do.'

And then she burst out crying again. Poor little Hildred, poor child!

That was a long, strange day. It seemed as if it ought by rights to be mid-day, when the sun had only been up for an hour or two, and it was difficult to understand how other people could be quietly waking up to their every-day business.

My father was having his breakfast. A few labourers were going across the bridge to their work. A flock of sheep with a cloud of dust round them, moved slowly along the road on the way to their pasture. Even Granny, with the tears all gone and her face as placid as if it had never been ruffled, was stirring about her morning's work.

'I wonder where poor Cuthbert'ill be now,' she said at dinner time; 'miles away by this time, I reckon. You'll be feeling a bit down-hearted, Willie, sure, without him.'

I felt rather more than a bit down-hearted, but it was no good telling Granny so.

'Well, it does seem strange to think that the lad's really gone,' she said again; 'don't it now, Stephen?' My father gave a sort of grunt that might mean anything. After dinner, as he stood by the chimney-piece, his eyes fell upon a many-clasped knife that belonged to Cuthbert. He looked round to see if any one was watching him; presently his fingers closed quietly over it, and it was dropped into his pocket. I took no heed, it was growing upon him, that habit of secretly hoarding any stray thing that came in his way.

Then began a time about which there is little to tell. Our life, except that Cuthbert was gone, moved on, seemingly unaltered. And yet the old time and the new were as different really, as a place that you have known in the sunshine looks when you see it again by moonlight. The place itself is unchanged, the outlines, the shape, the substance are still there, only the colouring is gone. All that gave warmth and brightness has been taken away. Grey and black and white tints alone remain.

Was it really only yesterday that I had come home, I thought—only yesterday that I was watching a sunset of clear gold and red in a blue sky, as I came along the road from Morechester, thinking my sunlit thoughts? In an hour or two I was to see Hildred. Home where she was, lay somewhere in the heart of that bright west.

When I reached the village the sun set for me indeed. The light faded in a minute from my cloudland of dreams.

The time hung all the more heavily on my hands, that I was too lame, for a while after my coming home, to be able to do much. It was a great comfort when I got strong again. Hard work, work that lasted from morning until night, was the best thing then. I did not care to think more than I could help. It only made things worse.

At first I could not make out rightly, how much or how little it was my duty to be with Hildred, remembering that now she was only a charge left to me by Cuthbert. It would have been easier to keep away altogether, but the poor child was unhappy. In the newness and strangeness of her first sorrow, she needed a great deal of comforting. No one had much time or thought to give to the remembrance of Cuthbert, so she came to me, reminding me that I had promised to be good to her.

It has always seemed to me that any trouble is the most easily borne in silence. Many words only make the pain worse, and take away from the patience and strength with which one has to bear it. But it was different for little Hildred. Child-like, or woman-like, it was a comfort to her to say how very sad she was. She came to tell how she missed Cuthbert; how long and dull the days seemed without the hope of seeing him; of how she often thought she heard his voice calling to her, and forgot that it was gone far beyond her hearing.

Anyone that has loved and lost a friend knows well all that she felt. But to her it was just as strange and dreadful as if the world, since it began, had not been full of partings. It was so new to her to wake up in the morning, wondering what the weight upon her heart could be—so sorrowful, when everything was quiet, to cry herself to sleep.

We were not the only people in that part of the country who had cause to rue the visits of recruiting parties. There were the Moores, cousins of her own, whom Martha Clifford was never tired of holding up as an example. How often have I heard her exhort Hildred to patience, by telling her how much less to be pitied she was than the poor old Moores! Hildred did not think so, inasmuch as a new sorrow always seems worse than an old one, and the trouble that had come upon the Moores was of old standing now.

Three or four years ago their only son did, what Cuthbert had just done—enlisted, leaving his father and mother to get on as best they could without him.

It was hard on them certainly, for they were growing old, and had looked to David as the bread-winner for the future. 'If you knew what it was to want bread, Hildred,' said Martha, 'you would not have so much time for fretting about Cuthbert.'

I don't think it had come to the Moores wanting bread, but I remember well the talk of the country side, and how it was said the ferry-house over the Wynn would soon have other tenants, for an old man like Moore could never manage the ferry-boat by himself.

Certainly the river at the ferry ran very swift and strong, and the old boat was a heavy one. Moore's house, a tumble-down stone building, comfortable enough inside, but a bleak sort of place to look at, stood hanging over the river, at the corner where the road comes out of a winding pass through the hills and ends at the ferry. It was the only way the farmers and people living up in the hills had of getting to Morechester. The boat carried across many a load of cattle for Morechester Market, many a man and horse bound for the Market Cross. Still the place was so wild and unfrequented that passengers were rare things, and the ferryman often worked in his strip of garden, and tended his goats, for days together, without the boat being once called for. There it lay, chained just beneath the house, with its ponderous oars, as big, clumsy, and flat-bottomed a thing as you would wish to see.

Cuthbert and I knew it well in the days of our rambles over the country. We knew old Moore and Moore's wife, and Elfrida their servant-maid, and David the son, who got so tired of the ferry-boat, and the lonely house, and the noise of the river sweeping by, that he went for a soldier, and left the place more silent and deserted than before.

In time old Moore fell sick. It was then that they began really to miss David; for what was to become of them, now his father could row the ferry-boat no longer? Then Elfrida, their faithful maid, went down and unloosed the boat, and rowed it across herself, with her strong arms. And she told her old master and mistress not to fret, for she would do her best—they should not leave the old ferry as long as she had hands to serve them.

Elfrida—I remember her well—was a tall strong lass, with a grave, faithful-looking, kindly face, and a pair of steady brown eyes. Hers was a true heart and a stout arm. The old people had been good to her, and she was not going to leave them at their need. But it was a rough life for a woman, especially as winter drew on, and the wind blew wildly from the hills, and the river rose.

Farmers coming home late at night from Morechester Market, wanted to be ferried across, and it was bitter work unchaining the boat and pushing out into mid-stream in the darkness. Elfrida grew to dread the shout and whistle from the other side, that summoned the ferry-boat to go across, but she never said anything. It had to be done, and she was glad to think of the old couple, comfortable under their own roof, often in bed and asleep, not knowing that she was pushing the boat along across the black river, with the rain dashing in her face, and the current striving against the whole strength of her arms, to sweep the boat down-stream.

One night, a very stormy night in November, Elfrida heard the unwelcome call come across the water. The wind and the rush of the stream almost drowned it; still there it was, and often repeated, as if the owner of the voice was getting impatient. So she lighted her lantern and pushed off, guiding the boat as well as she could by the rope that was stretched across the river. Her passenger was a farmer going home from Morechester, and as he led his horse into the boat Elfrida saw that he walked unsteadily. She was used to that sort of thing on market days, but to-night, as they started to cross back again, the man was pulling at his horse, making it move restlessly. Elfrida spoke sharply, bidding him be still and keep the horse quiet. The farmer answered angrily, and moved suddenly from his place—the boat rocked—there was a sudden splash in the water, a loud cry, and he was gone.

Elfrida knew that the current was running swiftly, and that a moment would carry him beyond help. She did not stay to think, but plunged in after him. She was a brave swimmer, and a brave woman, but the stream was hurling along, and the night was dark. What came after the shock of the chill water she could never quite tell. She knew that she clutched the man's hair as he rose, and then all the rest was confusion, until she felt someone dragging them both up the bank, and saw lights flashing in her eyes. Another party of homeward-bound farmers had come up, and pulled them in, but not until she had struggled with her burden close to the shore.

That night's deed made Elfrida famous in the country round. People went all the way from Morechester to look at her; but she remained just as simple as ever, rowing her boat quietly, and speaking little to any one.

It fell out strangely enough, that David Moore belonged to the regiment which our Cuthbert entered. They met in the barracks when Cuthbert first joined, and sailed in the same ship for India. We heard of their being together from David's wife. One evening Elfrida, going across to fetch a passenger who had called for her, found a little woman waiting at the river's edge, with a bundle in her arms, who said that she was David's wife. He was gone to India and had sent her home to his father, and here was Baby.

Elfrida thought in her heart that they had hard work enough to keep themselves, and now here was David, instead of coming back to help, sending his wife and child home to be a burden. She rowed the stranger across silently, and when they landed took the bundle in her arms—and it was Baby. Ah, well, perhaps twice in a lifetime one may see as beautiful a child as baby was. Loose tumbled curls that looked like gold, shone on Elfrida's eyes out of the bundle—eyes like periwinkles, bright blue stars, she said, looked straight up and smiled at her. A pouting rosebud of a mouth laughed outright, and baby put out a firm round dimpled hand to clap her on the cheek.

All in a moment Elfrida's heart bowed down before its lord and master. 'Here is something to work for, early and late, night and day,' she thought to herself; but she did not say so, only she clasped the bundle that had suddenly grown so precious, tightly in her arms, and carried it into the house.

Henceforward baby reigned like a king at the ferry, by right, I suppose, of his crown of golden locks.

So Elfrida worked on with a will; David's little London-bred wife sat indoors with the old people, and both they and we thought of the soldier laddies who were away at the wars.

Day by day I talked to Hildred about Cuthbert, and told her how proud she would be of him when he came home safe from the wars. And Hildred believed all I said. It was easy to comfort her for the moment, only the next day it was all to do over again. I used to build gorgeous castles in the air for her, feeling all the time that it would half break my heart to see any of them come true. Yet there was a pleasure too in watching Hildred, listening with her eyes bent down, and the long dark lashes that made her face look like a cloudy day sweeping her cheeks despondently. And when at last she raised them it was just as if the sun came out suddenly. She was like a child to talk to. I sometimes thought, what a slight thing she was for two strong men to have set their hearts upon.

And thus a long time slipped away. Cuthbert left us in the summer, and winter was well on before Hildred got her first letter from him. That letter, written at sea and sent home by a vessel which met theirs, how much we all thought of it!

We stood round Hildred, waiting for news, as she held the big brown letter in both hands, eager, flushed, and laughing, yet half unwilling to break its great red seal. She unfolded it slowly and read it out, her finger pointing along the lines. It was a beautiful letter—everybody said so—and yet how little it told us about him! It left him well, he wrote, and he liked a soldier's life, but he often remembered home, and thought of his own true love by night and day. And he sent his kind respects to all inquiring friends. That was all.

In time, the letter too became a thing that had come long ago, and the winter dragged on into spring. Hildred grew slowly more accustomed to Cuthbert's absence, and I knew better what a hard task it was that he had left me.

I missed my brother Cuthbert sorely. I had never loved him more than since he took from me unwittingly that which I cared for most in life. With him all the life and cheeriness of our house had gone away—we who remained were so grave and old.

Indeed Granny, the oldest of the three, was the most talkative, perhaps the happiest. The twilight of her life was closing round her, and, looking back over the long way she had come, she could talk cheerfully over what had once troubled her the most, but which now lay dimly remembered in the distance behind her.

Sometimes she reminded me of my mother, by the expressions which she used. And I thought Mistress Dorothy was right when she said that there is a language which the great Master teaches to all his scholars, different as they may be to one another, and that it grows the more easy to them the nearer they are to leaving school and being taken home to their Father's house.

'Stephen will be vexed,' Granny said, 'to think that I should go; but it's quite time, Willie, and I shall be glad;' and she went on, lay-ing her hand on mine, 'To think of me, my dear, poor me, with a golden crown upon my head!'

Dear old Granny, with the white hair under her mob-cap, and her withered, aged face. Ah, well! would not all the lines be smoothed away before the crown of life was laid upon her brow?

It may be that my father saw her failing, and was 'vexed' by it, but he said nothing. Besides, Granny toiled that he should still find a bright fire and tidy room to greet him, and Hildred was always com-ing in to help her. Granny said the sight of her sweet face made her feel young again. 'Her cheeks are like the red roses that grew over our porch when I was a girl. They used to say I was like one of those roses once, for I was a pretty girl, my dears, though you would not believe it now. I don't think girls are so pretty now-a-days as they used to be when sister Nancy and I were young.'

'I am sure they are not, Granny,' Hildred would say laughing, and putting her red-rose cheek fondly against Granny's wrinkled face. 'Do you want me to do anything more this evening?'

'Bless you, pretty child, no. Run away with Willie. Young folks will ever be courting, and it's right they should—quite right.' And Granny nodded wisely. I felt the blood coming up into my cheeks.

'I think Granny sometimes mixes me up with Cuthbert,' I said.

'Perhaps she does,' Hildred answered. 'Yes, she is growing very old.'

One day my father chanced to be by when Granny was putting away the tea things, a task she never let any one take from her for fear of accidents. 'Young folks are careless at times, poor dears.' But Granny's steadiness of hand was not so great as her good will, or else her eyes failed her, for presently a cup fell down and was smashed to pieces. She looked startled, sorry, and half-frightened, as she found my father close behind her, and she gave up the rest of the cups to him quite meekly.

'Yes, Stephen, I see. You needn't talk about it. I'm not fit to do it any more. The children'll have to do the best they can, and I'll just sit still and wait. Don't you be afraid.'

She went and sat down in the chimney-corner, and twirled her thumbs rapidly one over the other. By-and-by the vexed look went out of her face, and the patience that made it quite beautiful came back.

'Where's Hildred?' my father asked me, after vainly trying to join the pieces of the broken cup together with his big fingers.

I said she had gone home.

'You should ha' married the girl, Will,' he said roughly, 'and have saved all this breaking and wasting. And then there would have been somebody to see to her,' motioning towards his mother.

'You know I couldn't.'

'I don't say as how you could then, but that's not now. Yon lad has forgotten her long since, I'll lay. They soldiers never hold to one thing long together.'

'Cuthbert forgotten Hildred!' I said. 'Not he.'

'Have it your own way,' he answered; 'only we want to get hold of some woman that'll keep things straight, that's clear.'

It was the first time for very long that he had touched on that old string. It was not by very many the last. The notion that I must bring home a wife, to 'keep things straight,' and to take care of Granny, had taken a strong hold upon him. If I was a fool, and would not marry Hildred, I must find just some one else; but he had far rather have her about the place than a stranger: he was used to the lass.

In vain I told him that she cared for Cuthbert, and would not marry me.

'Just you ask her. A bird in hand's worth two in the bush any day. Tell her I'll be a father to her.'

Once it might have been, not now.

I could only try my best to prevent him from missing any of his comforts, and turn my hand to everything. But I was clumsy: the woman's work did not come easily.

And now Cuthbert had been gone for more than two years. A second letter came from him some six months after the first. Since then we had heard nothing.

Of course no one could expect to hear often from those out-of-the-way parts of the world.

There were always plenty of good reasons to give Hildred, when she wondered, as she often did, why she never got a letter. But after months and months had passed away in silence, a thought of fear we did not like to face, which we tried to stifle and forget, began slowly to creep into our minds.

It seemed as if the clouds grew thicker as the third winter of Cuthbert's absence darkened over us.

My words of hope and reassurance lost the ring of truth: they did not comfort Hildred as they used to do.

'It's no good, Willie,' she would say. 'You can't make yourself believe it all.'

No more I could. Even to my own ears my reasoning sounded hollow and unsatisfying.

We knew that David Moore's wife had got a letter more than once since we had heard, but—it seemed strange, her husband never so much as mentioned Cuthbert's name. Whenever I could spare the time, which was not often, for it was a long and rough journey, I went over to the ferry, in the faint hope that they might have tidings for us. There was a sort of tie between us and this household, where also there was watching and waiting.

They did not watch as we did. They had less uncertainty, and perhaps more patience. Moore's quiet little wife never lost her placid look for long together, even though one of the letters she received was written by a comrade of David's, to tell her that he was wounded and could not write himself. He bade his wife not take on, for he was getting better, and she believed, and obeyed him implicitly. As for the old father and mother, their daily comforts were their first thought. The draught that came from the kitchen window, and the fine crop of potatoes in the garden, occupied them full as much as any fears for David. The pity that Martha Clifford still bestowed on the poor Moores was wasted. As long as they had Elfrida to work for them, they wanted nothing else.

What they would have done without her, no one could guess. Elfrida never told them that she might have left them at any moment, had she so willed it, for a comfortable home of her own. But so it was.

I used to watch her with great interest. The man whom she had saved from drowning did not forget what a debt of gratitude he owed her. He was for ever coming down to the ferry, only, it seemed, for the pleasure of being rowed over the river by Elfrida, and of staring at her all the way across.

Each time he tried to get through a set speech of thanks, that with much trouble he had put together, and each time he forgot it in the middle. It did not signify, for Elfrida took little heed of him. She told him once, that she had done but her duty, and that he had no call to thank her, and after that she wondered why he came so often, and ferried him quietly backwards and forwards all in the way of business.

He was a widower, the tenant of a small but thriving sheep-farm up yonder in the hills, where abode peace and plenty, much live stock, and many children.

Nothing was wanting but a mistress; and after a while he grew to think that Elfrida was one of the right sort, that she would make a kind mother to the children and a comfortable partner for himself.

The good man began to paint glowing pictures of the place he could take her home to, if she had but a mind to come. I don't think Elfrida turned quite a deaf ear. It did sound very pleasant—that well-to-do homestead, with the cows in the shed, and the poultry in the yard, the flocks on the hill-side, the dairy and the pigs. Elfrida felt kindly to the honest farmer in his best red waistcoat, who wanted to make her 'missus' of all these good things. And then how comfortable it would be never to have to cross the ferry on the winter nights that were coming round again, and to be able to put away for ever a certain passing feeling of uneasy wonder that had troubled her once or twice, as to what would become of her when she grew old.

Yes, that was all very well. Still there was Baby. She could never really think of leaving him. What would he do—poor little Davy—if she were gone? What would any of them do indeed? but that first question went nearest to Elfrida's heart.

After she had been listening silently all the way across, to the farmer's description of that place that must surely be very like Paradise, Elfrida lifted up her eyes, and there stood baby on the bank, clapping his hands and shouting at the boat. Baby, with a torn frock and a scratched face, and little bare muddy legs, yet beautiful exceedingly. Elfrida's heart gave a great thump, as it always did when she saw him. 'No, I never could leave Baby.'

'But I've got a baby too, up there at home,' the farmer pleaded.

She looked at him. 'Ah, but he's never like our Baby.'

The farmer scratched his head, and thought of his poor little chap at home, the thin, white-cheeked boy that never would thrive after his mother died and left him. Then he turned to Davy, and saw how his blue eyes shone, and how proudly he tossed back his yellow curls, and laughed his ringing laugh. And how Elfrida looked at him!

No, little Joe was not like that.

'Still, it seems a pity,' he said, 'don't it now, when things are so comfortable, as I've been telling you?'

Elfrida did not even hear him, for Davy, with the air of a king, was allowing her to carry him up the steep bank home to supper.

One day when I was there, the farmer brought down Joe to the ferry, with a kind of hope that the sight of Davy's little motherless rival might touch Elfrida's heart.

The visit did not turn out well. Davy made a bad beginning by knocking his guest down, without the smallest provocation except that he did not like him. Thereafter Joe's shrill cries of fear and anger could by no manner of means be hushed. He stood clasping his big daddy's leg with gasping sobs, a weak, pale-faced, poor-spirited little mortal. 'So-ho, Joe, quiet,' his father kept on saying, patting and smoothing him down, rather as if he had been a cart-horse.

Elfrida, on her side, was holding back Davy, trying to scold him, and make him beg Joe's pardon; but there he stood, nothing daunted, like a prince, Elfrida said, his head thrown back, his eyes sparkling, and one small fist doubled, ready as soon as he was released for another hit at poor terror-stricken Joe.

It did not do. Joe was taken home to the hills, without having greatly aided his father's cause, and the farmer was fain to fall back again upon patience as his best helper after all.

And indeed so were we. I had to go back to Wyncliffe that evening with the old answer, 'No, Hildred, no news yet.'

'I am so tired, so tired of waiting,' she said wearily.

She was standing on the hearth-stone, in the red light of the fire. The rest of the room was dark, for the early dusk of winter had gathered outside. Only the glow from the burning embers fell on her bent face and clasped hands.

Her words sounded all the more dreary that they were spoken in a lowered tone, for Granny, who of late had ceased to take much notice of anything, sat as usual, half asleep, in the chimney-corner.

But she must have heard in part, for she roused up suddenly, and asked, 'Who is tired? What is she talking of?'

We did not answer for a minute, and then I said, 'Only of Cuthbert, Granny.'

'Ay, Cuthbert. Is the lad here?'

'Oh Granny, no,' said Hildred, 'we wish—we wish he were.'

'He will come,' said Granny, raising herself up and speaking in a strange, clear tone. You will see him, never fear. It may be a long time first—' She looked through the firelight into the darkness beyond, as if her eyes were fixed on something that we could not see; 'a long time, but wait patiently, pretty child; wait, Willie. You will see him again.'

Hildred came close to me, and, half-frightened, laid her hand on my arm. We both stood looking wonderingly at Granny, from whose eyes the unaccustomed light was already fading away. The voice and look had given me an odd sort of thrill, and Hildred whispered, 'Willie, do you think she saw anything?'

'No—no—I don't think so. Granny.'

I spoke to her, and Hildred bent down and touched her, but she had sunk back again into the half slumber from which she had roused herself for those few minutes.

'Don't let us disturb her now,' Hildred said. 'We must do as she told us—wait. We will ask her again to-morrow.'

But when to-morrow came, our question remained unasked and unremembered. We only thought how her own long waiting was over, her hopeful patience changed into perfect joy. For Granny had gone from us. In the morning we found her lying with the winter light streaming across her face. We thought she was asleep. So she was. She had fallen into the quiet sleep of death.

One could scarcely call this a sudden sorrow, or a bitter sorrow. We had long known that it must come, and to her it was very welcome. Only we missed her. The chimney-corner looked empty, and we went in and out without the kindly, cheerful word that for so many years had been used to greet us. Granny had been very good to us.

Neither Hildred nor I could forget the words that she had spoken about Cuthbert on the last evening of her life. We looked upon them as a kind of prophecy. Without saying anything to one another, I believe we both began at that time to have a vague feeling that he was near to us—that he was coming home.

I know I never heard the bell ring at the Castle gate, without a quick thought that it might perhaps be him. I have seen Hildred stand by the half-hour together gazing at the bit of road by the bridge, where people coming from the village up to the Castle could first be seen. She got into a way of looking over her shoulder, and from side to side as she walked, as if she half expected that some one would appear from behind an angle of the broken walls, or from under the shadow of a tower. For the first time in her life she did not like to cross the ruins alone after nightfall.

'The girl seems as though she was living in a maze,' Martha Clifford said one day. 'I don't know what she would be at.' And she went behind Hildred unawares, and put her hand on her shoulder. Hildred gave a great start and turned round with the colour rushing into her cheeks.

'Why, child, what ails you?' her sister-in-law asked, not unkindly, 'that you stand there staring at nothing, and shake like a leaf if one does but touch you?'

'I don't know,' said Hildred, looking down again at the bridge, across which two people were moving slowly, and sighing as she saw them turn away along the river side.

The sun was setting in a frosty sky over the trees, and its red light shone through the bare branches and was reflected in the stream. It was Christmas Eve.

'Watching will bring no one back the quicker,' said Martha, 'and it's Christmas time. You'd better be merry with the rest, child.'

Hildred looked after her as she walked away with wistful eyes. 'Oh Willie,' she said, turning round to me, 'I should so like a merry Christmas. Everybody seems to be having one, all but us. And I thought maybe he would be let come home because it is Christmas, and then we should be merry too.'

'You must wait a little longer, Hildred.'

'That's what you always say; but I'm tired of waiting, and I want so much to be happy.'

It had seemed as if people were very merry in the village down yonder, to-day. The one shop-window was turned into a bower of holly and evergreens, stuck all about with oranges and rosy apples. To almost every house some one had come home to spend Christmas among their own folk. The village-green was full of pleased faces, and shouting children, and laughter, and glad greetings. Couple after couple of happy lovers had met Hildred, and wished her a merry Christmas as they passed; and though she gave the wish back heartily, yet each time the great longing to be happy like the rest swelled higher in her heart.

All day she had been working with the other boys and girls at dressing the little old grey church for Christmas Day. They had twined green wreaths round the thick short pillars and over the low arches, and a bunch of holly was stuck in each corner of the square pews. Under the east window, woven in shining holly leaves and scarlet berries, the words gleamed out, 'Behold we bring you glad tidings of great joy.'

They were the last thing that met Hildred's eyes as she turned under the porch, and looked back into the church. And her heart went out to meet them. Will it not be forgiven her, that in her sore longing for 'glad tidings,' she passed over their grand meaning, the mighty message of joy unto all people, and took them to herself as an omen that some good news was coming to her at last?

Christmas certainly is not always a merry time. Nay, often it is sadder than all the rest of the year; and yet I believe that people must be beginning to grow old before they quite give up an unreasonable half-formed idea that they have in some sort a right to be happier than usual at Christmas. Old custom has linked the words 'merry' and 'Christmas' together, and it is hard to put them asunder in our thoughts, though in action it is easily done.

There is a great deal that makes Christmas look and sound cheerful;—roaring fires in farm-house kitchens; holidays from school and work; larders well stocked with Christmas cheer; the church bells, that ring their merriest peals, chiming and pealing, and clashing out every change that the ringers can put together.

And the dear old carols; their quaint rhymes set to music full of odd flourishes, familiar since the childish days when we lay wide awake on Christmas night, listening breathlessly to the voices in the distance, and doubting whether the 'angelick host' of which they sang could have made more melodious music.

We were great at Christmas carols in Wyncliffe. Everybody that could sing—and some that only thought they could—went down to the schoolhouse, for the few weeks before Christmas, on the nights that the singers practised.

Cuthbert and I had been 'waits' ever since we were little schoolboys, with small shrill voices that were always being left behind when the tune swept up suddenly to a high note far above our reach, or rolled down into a manly grumble somewhere in the very heart of the bass. Standing close together and singing with might and main, we could not hear our own voices, but could only see each other's mouths wide open. Our childish piping was buried out of hearing beneath the rude deep men's voices, and the clear notes of the women, the scraping flourishes of the fiddles, and the tones of the flute that whistled and stopped, and lost its way, and found it again, when nobody was expecting it, like a gust of wandering wind.

Things improved for us as time passed on. I played the violin myself in these latter days, and for several years Cuthbert's voice made the fortune, and was the great boast, of the waits. It was a story often told, how a stranger, hearing us sing one Christmas night, turned out to be the organist of Morechester Minster, and wanted Cuthbert afterwards to join the choir of the great church. We did not wonder. It was but natural. What musician would not have wished for that sweet rich voice of his, that seemed to blend all the others together and bring them into harmony?

Ah, well, that was the Christmas before Cuthbert went away. We had learnt to do without him now. Nevertheless, the carols, like many other things, were no longer quite what they used to be.

Hildred and Matt Clifford and I had been round with the waits this year for several nights.

It chanced that I was late in joining them on the evening of Christmas Day, and as I crossed the village green my father met and stopped me.

'I say, lad, you haven't heard the news.'

There was light enough for me to see the strange, awed look on his face, and to feel that whatever the news was, it had shocked him, and made him half-unwilling, and yet eager, to tell it. Besides, he had just a shade of that triumph which people's faces wear when they have foretold that something has come to pass.

'That boy Cuthbert has got killed in the wars.'

I stood still and stared at him.

'Yes, he has got killed, poor lad,' my father repeated. 'Esther Reynolds brought the news. Young Moore, over at the ferry, has come home, and she had it from him.'

Had Hildred heard it? That must be thought of first of all. Would there be time to stop them from telling her suddenly?—Hildred, who sometimes fancied that he was coming home, that he was near to her.

Old Esther Reynolds knew it—the greatest gossip in the village, to whom the telling of a bit of news was as the breath of life. No thought for Hildred would keep her silent, if she had the chance of spreading such a story as this. There was not a moment to be lost.

It was a clear frosty night, and the stars were shining. Every distant noise sounded distinct and close at hand. My own footsteps rang on the frozen road.

Very soon I heard them singing, the well-known carol waxing louder every minute as I got near to them, sounding so strangely discordant to my ears, which were still tingling with the death news.

Voices were singing, and church-bells chimed, the stars gleamed and sparkled like silver fire over the living, busy, holiday-keeping world, and Cuthbert was dead.

For a minute I stood still and gathered breath. How was it possible to tell Hildred, whose voice I fancied I could hear already rising clear above the rest—how would it be possible to go on and tell her that her lover lay dead, killed, buried in a far distant grave? What would she say? How could she bear it, when the mere thought of the words that must be spoken were making my heart beat too heavily for speech? Need I say anything yet? Surely nobody would tell her to-night. I would keep near her, and when this singing, that was such a mockery, was over, perhaps some words would be given me, some words, if such there were, that would make the blow fall less cruelly.

But the next moment I started forward again. There was a confused murmur, a movement in the group; some of the people stopped singing, and then came a sudden, sharp, half-choked cry, and the music ceased altogether.

They had got a lantern; some one held it up, and the light fell on the face of Esther Reynolds standing there among them. I was too late.

Someone called out my name, and then Hildred, ghastly white in the cold star-light, turned and met me, with her hands stretched out before her.

'It isn't true! Willie, tell me it isn't true.'

'My poor Hildred!'

I took the hands so pitifully held out, but she snatched them away, throwing them wildly up into the air, and then with a long sobbing moan she fell down upon her knees.

The women gathered round her compassionately, and raised her up from the hard road, weeping with her, and trying to quiet her by kindly pitying words, of which she took no heed.

Esther Reynolds was wringing her hands, and saying over and over again, 'Oh poor lamb! I would not have told if I'd known she'd have taken on like this. What can I do for her, poor lamb?'

What could she do? What could any one do, but stand by helplessly, watching the poor child struggle through the first bitterness of her sorrow? No one could bear the blow instead of her, or ease her pain.

I daresay her brother Matt did what was the best for her. He laid his hand on her shoulder and bade her quietly come home. He had looked on in perplexed silence for the last few minutes, while he unscrewed his flute slowly, and put it away in his pocket. He did not try now to say anything comforting, but held his sister up in his strong grasp, for she was trembling too much to stand alone, and he led her away, her face hidden in her cloak.

There were no more carols sung that year at Wyncliffe. A blank silence fell upon those who were left. Presently some one said, 'Poor

Hildred!'

They asked who brought the news, and Esther dried her eyes and began eagerly to tell all she knew. I stood listening with the rest. It was not much to hear, though told in many words. David Moore had come back wounded from India, to his home at the ferry-house. He was in Cuthbert's regiment, and he brought word that Cuthbert had been killed.

'Poor Cuthbert!' said many sorrowful voices. They all loved him. Not one here but thought of him kindly, and had been friends with him in the days that were gone. And I. Oh Cuthbert, God knows I loved you, God knows I mourned for you, bitterly, bitterly.

It was ended then, the long hope, the fear we would not name, the watching for him who was never to come back. It was all over, and he was dead.

Dead! that was a hard thing to believe. For there was no farewell to remember, no day to look back upon as the last day of his life; no single parting word; only a great blank and silence in our thoughts. He had been, and he was not. That was all. We should never know for certain the day nor the hour when we lost him. Only on some day, long ago now, when thinking nothing, we were busy about our common work, he had been dying a soldier's painful death, with perhaps a farewell word for us in his brave heart, that would never reach us.

It had always seemed as if we feared so much, but we knew now how far stronger than our fears our hope had been. The blow could scarcely have fallen more heavily months ago, before we began to have the vague dread of evil that had darkened into utter night.

I thought it all over as I went slowly homewards, with a dull quietness that it was very strange to feel. I remembered him as a boy, and could recall his great love to me, without more than a numb heartache, and a feeling of wonder that I was not more unhappy.

I thought of a future in which I should be always lonely, and Hildred for ever broken-hearted, with a sort of pity for us both, as if I were but a looker-on at our lives.

And yet I envied Hildred; for when I went late at night to ask after her, they told me that she had sobbed herself to sleep. For the moment she had escaped from trouble, and her stormy sorrow all left behind, she had gone away into the land of dreams, where tears are not.

For me there were neither dreams nor sleep. All night I sat in my father's elbow-chair beside the fire, not caring to go to bed. At first the flames kept me company as they rose and fell and flickered, lighting the room fitfully. The stars shone in, glittering through the window. Then the fire died down to a dull glow. It grew black, with only a red spark here and there. It went quite out, and the room grew very cold. The night waned. A mist rose up and covered the stars. It became darker and darker. Then I suppose I fell asleep, for when I looked again, the grey chill of a winter's dawn was in the room. It was no longer to-day, but yesterday, that we heard of Cuthbert's death.

I dreaded seeing Hildred in her sorrow. It made me feel strange to her, as if I should not know how to greet her, and that instead of her familiar self, she would be to me as a mourner upon whom a great grief had newly fallen! Poor little Hildred. The strangeness all went away, and was forgotten directly we met, and she ran to me and held my hands, crying, 'Oh Willie, I wanted you. He belonged to you and me.'

'But I can't feel as if it could be true,' she said presently. 'I keep thinking all the time—of course it's foolish—that perhaps old Esther Reynolds made a mistake after all, and that David Moore meant some one else. Eh, Willie?'

I shook my head. 'But I can go to see him, and ask him about it,' I said, after thinking a little.

'Oh, will you? And ask him to tell us,'—her voice failed, and she shuddered,—'ask him whether it was great pain, and if it was soon over. I cannot bear to think he suffered long.'

Ah, Hildred! so you too had thought of those dreary questions that had been haunting me all night.

'I will go to-day,' I said. And that evening I was at the Ferry House.

It was generally a bleak place enough; but this afternoon winter sunshine was giving it a cheerful look, and a holly tree, brilliant with berries, made a bright spot of colour near the door.

They say trouble makes people selfish. I scarcely remembered until now that what brought us sorrow had filled this house with rejoicing.

The picture of home gladness that met my eyes as I went in, came upon me in sharp contrast with Hildred's tear-stained cheeks and heavy eyes.

Some one had stuck holly-branches all over the room, usually so bare. The fire blazed cheerily. On one side sat David Moore's little wife, quiet still, but with a smile of great contentment on her face, looking down at her husband, who sat on a wooden stool at her feet, with his arms resting on her lap and his eyes fixed on her.

There was a handkerchief bound round his head, and when he

turned round I saw that he would have looked very ill if it had not been for the radiant happiness that shone from his pale face. His mother, sitting close by, put out her hand every now and then, and touched his red coat to make sure it was really him. Even old Moore had roused up. And in the back-ground little Davy stood on the dresser with one arm round Elfrida's neck, a bunch of holly in his hand, and a scarlet handkerchief, in imitation of his father, twisted in his curly hair.

David Moore did not look like the bearer of evil tidings. The question I came to ask seemed sadly out of place among these happy people.

But there was a pause after they had greeted me, and then I had to ask it.

'You were with Cuthbert Franklyn in India?'

'Yes, I was.' He stopped a moment and then said more slowly, 'I suppose you know he's dead.'

It was true, then—quite true. I stood silent. Little Davy laughed merrily, and Elfrida stopped him with a grave 'hush.'

Presently Moore said—

'We lost ever so many fellows in our regiment, and I never looked to come home myself.'

His wife put her hand softly on to his head as he sat at her feet, and he looked up smiling, and forgot everything else.

'Where was it Cuthbert Franklyn died?' I asked at last.

'Killed at the battle of Conjeveram, fighting against Tippoo Saib, same day as I got this wound in the head.'

'You are sure? Did you see him after he was killed?'

'No, I got my wound early in the day. I was left for dead. They never thought I should have lived. I was a long time in hospital. When I saw some of our fellows again, after I was invalided home, they told me that Franklyn was among the missing.'

He could tell me no more than this. And I stood there, thinking sorrowfully over it. I felt that I brought a dreary silence over that happy party. David Moore and his wife spoke to each other in low voices. The old father fell asleep, and Elfrida carried little Davy out of the room.

I turned to go away; Moore followed me to the door, wished he had brought me better news, and said he would have come over to see his cousin Martha Clifford, but that his furlough was so short. Only three days to be with wife and child after this long time! So we shook hands, and he went back to his bright fireside.

It was too late to go home that night. The short winter's day was over before I left the ferry, and it was afternoon again, a dark, cold, Sunday afternoon, before I got to Wyncliffe next day.

The church-bells were still ringing for evening service when I came into the village. Hildred was to meet me at church, for the Vicar never liked the musicians to be away if they could help it, and I played the fiddle up in the gallery every Sunday.

Nearly everybody had gone in when I reached the steps leading up to the churchyard. Only Hildred was standing under the lych gate, and watching for me in the failing light.

If it had been good news I was bringing her, I should have quickened my steps when I saw her.

Now I did not look up, but walked slower, wishing that something would come to prevent my having to destroy the last hope she had.

I think she understood. She came two steps down towards me. The church-bells stopped ringing.

'Willie,' she said in a whisper.

I shook my head.

'Was it true, then?'

'All true.'

She drew back, covering her face with her hands, but she was very quiet. A blow in all its heaviness cannot fall twice.

We stood together for some minutes. She was shivering so, that I told her to go home, but she shook her head, and passed slowly, without speaking, under the church porch.

I went up into the gallery. It was the Sunday after Christmas, and the day had been so short that the light was already waning before the service began. This afternoon, too, a snow-storm was coming, and the heavy clouds made it duskier than usual. There were two faint lights glimmering over the reading-desk. When the last heavy footstep had sounded along the aisle, and there was silence through the church, it was almost out of darkness that the vicar's voice came, reading in a quiet even tone the opening words of the service: 'The sacrifices of God are a broken spirit; a broken and a contrite heart, O God, Thou wilt not despise.'

Broken hearts! It was good that God did not despise them, since there must be so many in the world.

* * * *

My father was anxious to be told all that David Moore had said. He asked me many questions, and listened to every word I could remember with an interest that would have puzzled me, but that my thoughts were so full of Cuthbert, that it seemed natural every one should be as much taken up about him as we were.

'Then Moore didn't say whether he was killed directly, or how long he lived after he got his wound?'

'No, Moore was hurt himself; he did not hear until long after.'

'How long?'

'Two or three months, I think, he said, when he got back to his regiment.'

'Well.'

'They told him that poor Cuthbert was among the missing.'

'Only missing,' said my father, leaning forward; 'not killed.'

I paused a moment. It had not struck me before.

'But then it's the same thing, for sure,' my father went on eagerly, 'quite the same thing. It's just the way they put it. I didn't mean to throw a doubt on his being killed, mind, Willie.'

'Moore did say missing.'

'Ay, missing or killed. 'Tis the same thing. Now don't you go and fash yourself for a word. The poor lad's killed, sure enough. There's no manner of doubt about that.'

He bent over and touched my arm, to enforce his words. I could see he was vexed with himself for having asked the question, and wanted to make me forget it.

'I suppose they would have known,' I said, after thinking over it, and the hope that had glimmered for an instant went out again—not quite, though. The certainty was shaken since it had been questioned; and yet David Moore had seemed to have no doubt. 'He's dead, you know;' I remembered his words well.

'To be sure they knew,' said my father, watching me, as I saw, 'I've thought myself how it would be this long time past. I never looked to see him come home again.'

My father seldom troubled himself to speak so much. It was almost too much for the object he wanted to gain, of lulling my doubts to rest. By-and-by, he said rather hesitatingly, 'I say, lad, you wouldn't go and tell Hildred what we've been talking of. It'll just unsettle her again for nothing.'

The more he tried to undo the impression he had made on me, the less I was able to forget it. It was a small seed of doubt that, sown unawares, was to live and come up after many days. Try as I would in after times I could not root it out. There it was, too shadowy to be met and fought with outright, too real to be disregarded.

I can scarcely tell what feeling prompted me to tell Hildred. It seemed right to do so. But she scarcely took it in.

'Killed or missing, it's about the same,' my father told her, and Hildred's eyes, raised with a look of eagerness, sank again listlessly. 'I suppose it is,' she said sighing.

I said no more then. It was better for her that the wearing suspense should be at an end. And after all, was there any real ground of hope? I believed, though I could not feel, that Cuthbert was dead.

'If only I had seen him, to say good-bye,' Hildred said, 'I think I could bear it better. I wish he were buried in the churchyard, where we could go and see his grave.'

Ah! I wished so too. That silent darkening down of fear had been very dreadful, but the fitful glimmer that was most likely false, but that would gleam out now and again, from among the ashes of our dead hopes, was to my mind more dreadful still.

* * * *

These were the thoughts of many months.

I find that it is not easy to tell one's story. You may mean to tell it all, yet you find that the greater part you have left out altogether.

For so many things go to the making up of a man's life. It is not all sweet nor all bitter. There is in it much brightness, and more shadow, and a great deal besides that is neither cloud nor sunshine, neither bitterness nor sweetness, which fills up the measure of each passing day. One wave does not make a river—rather many; some dance and sparkle, touched by the sunlight from above, while all the time the under-current is flowing sorrowfully on.

And we were busy about many things apart from Cuthbert, were glad and sorry, anxious and hopeful, had plans and thoughts, cares and pleasures, that had nothing to do with him. Still the thought of him lay beneath it all.

It was a busy year for me at Furzy Nook; for as Farmer Foster grew older I had of course more and more on my hands. Time passed wonderfully quick—Sunday after Sunday marking off a week that ended before I had thought of it as much more than begun. We could let the weeks go as they would now, without counting every one as a fresh link in a chain of waiting. There was nothing to wait for, or to hope for any longer. So they all said.

It was better for Hildred that it should be so.

After that dark winter was past, she began to brighten with the spring. She was no longer the merry careless child she used to be. All that was over. But the flower that the rain had beaten down, lifted its head again slowly.

It was not that she had any thought of seeing Cuthbert again. Her last hope died on that Sunday after Christmas Day. No one was of the same mind as I was. Everybody called him 'poor Cuthbert,' and spoke of him as dead—everybody, odd to say, excepting good old Farmer Foster. Directly he heard my doubts he went far beyond me, into a perfect certainty of hopefulness. 'We shall have him home up-on us, never fear, before we know where we are,' he used to say; and as I walked beside his pony over the Furzy Nook fields, he told me again and again the same half-forgotten story, the end of which he never could remember, about some prisoners who escaped out of a French prison when he was a lad. I repeated the story, such as it was, to Hildred, but it did not cheer her. I thought she looked rather more grave than usual afterwards. 'Catching at straws still, Willie,' she said, shaking her head.

I suppose it was another straw I caught at later in the summer. One market-day at Morechester, as I stood near the Cross, I heard the ill-omened sounds of fifes and drums, and presently a recruiting party marched down on us from the High Street. It carried me back in a moment to that evening three years ago. I almost seemed to see the purple sky above the village street, and the lights shining through the inn-windows, and then the ribands in Cuthbert's hat, as the loud voice of the recruiting sergeant sounded in my ears.

No wonder that I recalled it so vividly, for as they drew near, I saw that this was the same man who had enlisted Cuthbert. I knew his upright figure and broad good-humoured face directly. The peo-ple round were laughing at the very same jokes that I remembered hearing in the street of Wyncliffe.

I made my way up to him in the crowd. He had seen Cuthbert after we had, and might somehow know what had become of him. There were two lads near him staring up in open-mouthed admira-tion of his scarlet coat and soldierly stride.

He turned away from them to me. 'No, I don't want to enlist,' I said, in answer to the accustomed speech. 'I am come to ask you a question. Do you mind one Cuthbert Franklyn, that you enlisted here three years ago?'

He shook his head with a loud laugh. 'If I'd got to remember half their names, my fine fellow, I'd need to have a good memory. Move on, will you?'

Walking on beside him I managed to tell him hurriedly, what we had heard of Cuthbert. 'Was there a chance of his ever coming back?'

'Why not?' he answered, in his careless, jolly voice. 'I don't know why he shouldn't. We're not all killed, you see, that go for soldiers. Ah! it's a fine life, my lads,'—this to the two boys who were still following him. 'No life like it,' and so on.

Those lightly-spoken words of his, the only ones of encouragement I had ever heard, fell upon me like a blow, and struck me speechless.

'Then you think that he may be living yet,' I asked again, presently.

'You there still!' He looked back good-humouredly. 'Well, there's no knowing. I can't say.'

'He was reported missing.'

'Ah! reported missing, that sounds bad. Still, I've known stranger things come round. Where was he killed, say you?'

'At the battle of Conjeveram, I think they called the place.'

'Conjeveram—seems to me I've heard a talk of prisoners taken there, but the outlandish Indian names are all alike. It's a chance, I tell you. Now, then.'

He had no more time for me. I went home with a beating heart, to tell Hildred. She was sitting in the honeysuckle-shaded porch of Clifford's house, spinning. The bees hummed in the sunshine, the waterfall splashed, Clifford's children were shouting at the river's edge, and Hildred was singing a low murmur of song that blended with the whirr of her wheel and the buzzing of the bees.

'Hildred,' I said, going up to her, 'I have seen Cuthbert's recruiting sergeant, and he thinks he may be alive.'

Hildred started, her hand fell, and the thread broke.

'He does not see why he should not come home some day,' I went on.

She got up, very pale.

'Cuthbert alive!' she said, dreamily. 'Where is he?'

'Oh Hildred, I don't know; I only said he might be living still.'

'Didn't you say he was coming?'

'No, no, it might be just possible.'

Hildred burst out crying.

'What's all this?' said Martha Clifford, coming up with a pail of water on her head. 'What's Hildred crying for?'

'I gave her a fright,' I answered repentantly, and I told Martha what I had heard and said.

'Dear me, Willie, leave the girl alone, do,' said Martha roughly. 'Don't begin all that over again. We had enough of it before we knew he was killed; watching and worrying, worrying and watching, from morning till night. Let bygones be bygones.'

'But I can't forget——'

'Well, others can if you can't. Let the dead rest, Willie Lisle.'

'If we could be quite sure——'

'And so you ought to be. It's all a whimsey you've got into your head. Cuthbert's dead enough, poor lad, but it's my belief you wouldn't be satisfied if you had seen him buried down yonder with your own eyes.'

'Don't, Martha,' said Hildred, brushing away her tears and coming to my side.

'It's enough to vex a saint,' Martha went on, 'let alone me, just when the girl was beginning to leave off fretting, and to take hold a little. I won't have it done, and so I tell you, Willie.'

'I wouldn't harm Hildred,' I said sorrowfully, 'but she and I can't forget; after what grandmother said before she died, and all. You mind that, Martha.'

Martha gave a sort of moan.

'It's only that he's more faithful than any of us,' said Hildred.

'Well, let him be faithful by himself. I won't have him coming upsetting everything, and you breaking your thread, Hildred, and going on like that. I'm ashamed of you.'

Hildred did look so pale for a time after this, that I saw Martha was right in part, and that I ought not to have spoken when there was nothing real to tell. She was rough-spoken, was poor Martha, but she was a just woman. No one ever could have a better neighbour, as we proved that next winter.

It was a hard winter. The snow came early, and lay long; the river, for the first time in many years, was frozen over. I suppose I noticed the cold more for my father's sake. All the autumn he had been ailing, but he would not give in as long as he could keep about. When Christmas came he was lying between life and death in a rheumatic fever.

We never thought he would see another spring, but somehow he struggled through it, and by March he was downstairs again, changed, and aged, and bent, but still a wonder, even to the doctor himself.

Martha Clifford and Hildred nursed him as if they had been daughters of his own, and he was 'ill to nurse,' as the old women say. Martha never got a word of thanks from him for all her goodness, but sometimes he laid his hand kindly on Hildred's head, and smiled at her.

It was pretty to see her trying to cheer him as he sat, hour after hour, with his eyes fixed gloomily on the fire, beating his stick slowly on the floor and saying nothing. It was a hard thing for him to believe, what his stiff aching limbs yet told him too plainly, that he would never be fit for any work again. Hildred did not lose patience, even with his darkest moods. Perhaps she guessed that they were darker still whenever she was away from him.

One wet blowy evening in that same month of March, I chanced to be kept much later than usual at Furzy Nook. Long before I got home it had grown dark, though I made as much haste as I could, thinking that my father's fire would have gone out, and that he would be tired of being by himself.

But when I lifted the latch, the firelight was shining cheerfully through the room, and Hildred sat on the wooden stool at my father's feet. I remember standing still for a moment to watch them. My father's head was bent down, and he was talking to her. Hildred sat looking up at him, her chin on her hand, and the fire lighted both their faces.

It looked so comfortable to see her there—so comfortable and homelike, sitting beside our fire, and keeping my father company. If I had known that I should find her when I came in from the stormy darkness, she, whom once I used to fancy would be always there with us!

My father looked round as I came in, but Hildred's face was turned away from me, and she did not see me. She gave a great start and stood up hurriedly when I touched her shoulder.

'Did I frighten you?' I said; 'you ought to have gone home, Hildred, before it came on to rain like this.'

'Does it rain?' she asked, without looking up.

The wind answered her, as it dashed the rain in a noisy gust against the window.

'You will get wet,' I said, watching her putting on her cloak and hood.

'I don't mind. I only waited because your father was alone, and I didn't like to leave him. I must go home now.'

'Thank you, my dear,' my father said. 'I wish you had not got to go home, but that you could stay here with us always.'

It was my father's way to say things like that to Hildred. They were hard to bear—hard to be reminded of what might have been—hard to listen to, and to say nothing.

I must let her go out now into the rainy darkness. I could never keep her—never—safe sheltered in the warmest corner of our fireside.

As my father spoke, Hildred bent down, still hurriedly, to bid him good night. He kept her hand, and said, 'Hildred, lass, will you come home here, and stay for always? Will you be my daughter?'

I took a step forward and laid my hand on Hildred's arm to draw her back. What was my father saying? He looked up at me and did not let go her hand. 'No one has been so faithful to you as he has. Won't you let him bring you home at last?'

Hildred could scarcely have heard the last words. The door closed behind her almost before they were spoken. I did not try to follow her, though she had gone out alone into the storm. I saw her put her hands over her face as she went out, to hide her tears.

'Father, what have you done?'

He had taken up his pipe and was lighting it slowly. It seemed strange that he should look at me so quietly in my great doubt and pain.

'No harm, lad, no harm. I should be glad to see you comfortable with her before I die.'

'Comfortable! With Hildred!'

'Ay, with my little Hildred. She's a good girl, and she'd make a good wife. Besides, I've always said as how it's lonesome without a woman about the house.'

I tried to speak quietly. 'Were you talking about me when I came home?'

The pipe was alight now. He never could be got to talk when he was smoking. He just answered 'Yes,' and no more.

'You didn't tell her all I once told you?'

'Why not? I've a mind to bring you and her together.'

'Father,' I said, 'you have forgotten Cuthbert and my promise.'

He made no reply for a few minutes, and then, as, he knocked the ashes out of his pipe, he said, 'Cuthbert's dead.'

I leant my head down upon my arm, without the heart to-night to go over the old ground.

'Well!' said my father at last, when the pipe was out and the fire had almost smouldered away.

I shook my head. 'Cuthbert trusted me, and after all he may be living yet.'

'Not he.' He took his stick, and as he got up slowly from his arm-chair to go to bed, he added, 'You should think a bit of Hildred, too, Willie.'

'Of Hildred!'

'She gave Cuthbert up for dead long ago, and she sees you most-ly every day.'

With that he went upstairs, leaning on my shoulder, and would not say another word except 'Good night.'

Good night! as if I could sleep with all this in my mind. Then Hildred knew now how I loved her, not as Cuthbert's brother, not as her old playfellow, but with a love as strong, as deep, longer far than his had been.

And she? Until now, whenever I believed, as sometimes I did, that Cuthbert was dead, my only thought had been that at some time in the years to come, when we knew all for certain, I might comfort her—that she might get to care for me, not as she had cared for her first love, but gradually a little, because I loved her so much, and so that she might grow at last to be content.

And now to be told, as my father had told me to-night, that I ought to think of Hildred's happiness. Was it possible that her happiness could depend the least on me? Could it be that her hope of seeing Cuthbert again was gone, and that her love had faded with her hope? She was so young—scarcely eighteen—when he left her. Her gentle nature was not made to stand alone. It might be that in its loneliness her heart had turned, without her knowing it, to the guardian who strove so hard to hide his love for her.

The rain was still pattering against the window, and the wind blew in gusts through the ruins, but I took no heed of the storm. I was happy. I think that hour, sitting alone in the chimney-corner, while the last sparks were dying out of the peat fire, was the happiest of all my life. For I only thought of Hildred, of how perhaps some day she would come and turn all my life into brightness. I had never dreamed, since Cuthbert went away, that she could ever care for me, and now what a dream it was! I remember it because it never came to me again, because I woke suddenly and the dream was gone. I do not know where it took me, or how long it lasted, but in it Hildred was my own. We were together. Then suddenly it seemed as if Cuthbert stood before me, and I could not meet his eyes, full of a grave reproach as he looked from me to Hildred.

My promise! I got up and paced the room with rapid steps—that cruel promise. Was I never to be free from it? All my life was it to drag me back from happiness and bind me fast in misery? If it was broken, what worse could come of it than this? It would not haunt me any longer then. No one would reproach me—no one would suffer by it. At all events I must take my chance of that. A broken promise! Why, it was not fit to weigh for a moment against the happiness of two whole lives. I should forget it, I must, surely in a little while; if not, who cared?

A whole storm of dark thoughts came sweeping over me;

thoughts that I cannot recall even now without a shudder—anger against Cuthbert—bitter rebellion against my fate—a mocking contempt for myself that I had kept the promise sacred hitherto. What promise ever held true? I thought. Master Caleb's old puzzle came back to me,—how the cup of water that was given in Christ's name was in no wise to lose its reward; yet it had caused my mother's death, and following step by step, from that one act came all my troubles. That had proved false then, like all the rest, false as I was myself. Did it prove false? The very saying of the holy Name—the sacred words—the remembrance of my mother's trustful face—of Dorothy's quietly-spoken confidence—all this calmed me, and in the black darkness I fell suddenly on my knees, and said—

'Oh, Mother's God, who wert to her a sure refuge, come now and help me!'

As I prayed, a strange feeling came upon me that my prayer rose up even into the presence of a merciful listening God. The storm did not cease, the trouble was not rolled away, but there came a little rift into the dark clouds over me, a little speck of light shone through the blackness, as if a voice said, 'Oh, thou poor soul, be comforted; I will help thee!'

I think that was my first real prayer.

The next day was Sunday. The storm had quite passed over before the sun rose, and the grass sparkled with silver rain-drops. The river swept past beneath, with a fuller flow; the robins made the air bright with their merriment, rejoicing that, as they hopped from twig to twig, they shook down showers of lazy brilliant drops from off the boughs.

It seemed strange that such a storm could pass, and leave no deeper traces behind.

Over my life, too, a storm had come last night, but it was followed by no sunny morning. I was quieter, however, for my mind was made up. Weary with much thinking I put off until the afternoon that which I felt I ought to say to Hildred.

She, and Clifford's two boys, Robin and Walter, walked home together after church, and little Jock and Phillis were with me. As we passed under the yew tree, I asked Hildred to stay with me for a few minutes. The children went on, and Hildred and I were both silent, listening to their merry voices as they died away. I did not know what to say first.—At last I asked her abruptly, if she remembered how Cuthbert bade her good-bye here.

She said yes, she remembered it quite well.

I took her hand and said—I know my voice was trembling—'You

have not forgotten him!'

'Oh no,' she answered; 'poor Cuthbert!'

'Sister!'—I had never called her by that name before—'when he went away he left you to me to take care of, and he asked me to talk about him to you, that you never might forget him. We have not spoken of him lately as often as we used, but it has not made any difference. If he were to come back he would find us just the same.'

She was silent.

'Eh, Hildred?'

'I shall always remember him,' she said in a low voice.

'And watch for his coming back?'

'Oh Willie, poor Cuthbert is dead.'

'Don't say that, Hildred—don't think it. I know that every one here believes it, but I don't. Some day we shall see him again.'

She sat down on the bank, with her hands, which she had clasped together, lying listlessly in her lap. I saw she did not share in my belief, and when I repeated 'He will come back to you,' she only shook her head.

'But at least'—I asked the question almost in a whisper—'at least you love him the same as ever?'

'It all seems so long ago,' she said, simply.

I turned away, angry with myself that the words gave me such a thrill of pleasure—almost angry with her for making me unfaithful. We were both false to him, for I had let her forget him.

'Oh Hildred,' I said, not speaking as I felt, 'and he loved you so dearly.'

My voice must have been very reproachful, though in truth the reproach was against myself, not against her, poor child. The tears came into her eyes, but she only repeated what she had said before: 'It does seem so very long ago.'

I did not know how to go on. For a time neither of us spoke. At last she said, 'Is it very wrong of me?'

'Wrong, Hildred! no,' I answered sadly. 'You were so young when he left you, that I suppose it was too hard for you to remember. Only, how could we meet him if he came back?'

She looked frightened. 'You don't really think he will.'

'God only can tell that—we must do everything as if we expected him. I know that if he were here it would be all right; you would only need to see him again. But Hildred'—I had come now to the most difficult thing I had to say,—'Hildred, my father told you, last night, something about me, that I never meant you to hear. It must be, for both of us, as if it had never been told.'

'Is it true?' she asked, without looking up.

'Yes.'

After a little while I said, 'Don't let it come between us. Let me be your brother still, and Cuthbert's.'

Hildred tried to say, 'Thank you.' Her tears were falling down slowly upon the clasped hands in her lap.

'Don't cry, dear, don't be sorry.'

'You have been so good to me,' she whispered.

They were very simple words. I don't quite know how it was, that I knew from them that she had grown to love me. I bent down, pressing my hands tightly together to force back the rising words.

Hildred that saw it was hard for me. She touched my arm with her hand, saying softly, 'Never mind me, Willie; I will try to be very good.' But her voice failed again, and she drew a long sobbing sigh. 'Oh, I am so tired—so tired of being unhappy.'

Harder still then—too hard. She was not made to bear trouble, but to be loved and taken care of. She scarcely seemed to understand now, why I could not comfort her as I always had hitherto.

The longing to take her home and try to make her happy, was stronger than I could bear. I could not be faithful to Cuthbert any longer. He was dead—again and again some voice whispered it in my ear. I believed it at last. He was dead, and he would never know. My first duty was to Hildred, for surely time and death had released me from my promise, and I knew now that she cared for me more than she had ever cared for him.

I knelt down beside her. I began to speak. What saved me? I scarcely know. Suddenly, far off in the evening stillness, some one began to whistle. My thoughts flew back to Cuthbert.

I went away from Hildred and leant over the wall, with my head resting on my arms. It was last night's battle over again, but harder, inasmuch as I knew Hildred's feeling now. I felt that upon my doing right depended more than the happiness of her life and of my own. I have heard that men have two angels, an evil and a good, who follow them through life. It seemed to me that they were both beside me then. But the good angel's shining eyes were growing sorrowful and dim, and the other (oh, why did it take a shape like Hildred's to tempt me) put out a hand to draw me nearer. Almost in despair I tried to pray. Those words—earliest learnt, and most familiar in all the world—the blessed words of Our Lord's Prayer, with its petition to be delivered from evil and temptation, came to my lips, and I repeated them.

Just then—it seems but a small thing—the whistle sounded again nearer at hand. Loud and clear came to my ears, Cuthbert's favourite old tune 'Over the hills and far away.' In a second it brought him before me, not as the distant soldier we had thought of as dead—not as Hildred's lover—but as my own boy-brother, the dear old Cuthbert of our happy days. All my love for him rushed back. I thought how unfaithful I had been to him, and my tears fell like rain down on the old wall.

So help had come. A second time God's mercy won the battle for me, even against myself.

After a time I went back to Hildred and took her hand. I cannot tell you what I said to her, but I wondered at myself for being able to speak so quietly. I told her how I had loved her all her life—not many words about that, for I had found that I could not trust myself, but I reminded her of the trust we held together, and that Cuthbert had left his heart fearlessly in her hands and mine. And I said, 'We must not fail him. To be true and faithful will be better for you, and happier too, dear, in the end.'

Hildred took her hand from mine, but she did not speak. Only, when I had said all I could, she whispered, 'Good-bye, Willie,' and turned to go away.

'Hildred, you understand me,' I could not help saying. She looked back, trying hard to smile, but her lips quivered sadly. She said, 'I am sure you know best, Willie.'

And then she left me.

* * * *

In the years that I have led a wandering life, it has been my fate to hear many stories told. From wayfaring men, whose path has led them for a time to journey with me—from travelled folk—from old people, to whom (as after this you will know well) the memory of their youth and the sound of their own voices is ever dear—from young ones full of themselves and of the world, that is still new to them—from all these I have heard many a tale.

In the summer twilight, when the stars are brightening—on lonesome roads where there is little to speak of or to look for, except the mile-stones—in crowded towns, I have listened to story after story. Oftenest of all, beside some friendly fireside, on a winter's night such as this is. The best stories come out then, the longest and the strangest, sometimes the saddest. I have been reckoned a good listener in my day. It is not easy to be weary, hearing of human hopes and fears, of human hearts and troubles.

114

But what I wanted to say just now is this: I have seen that the best story-tellers, those that get the most rapt listeners, put a great deal of change into what they tell. They are fond of passing suddenly from one thing to another, a sad bit, then a bright bit—a sunny day and then a stormy night. They make you cry one minute, and the next you are laughing with them. And so they go on, black and white, light and shade, for ever. I hope you will forgive me that I do not know how to do this. It must be the right thing in a story, since it succeeds so well, but I cannot see that it is thus in nature. The sunshine and the shadow do not fall by rule, one following the other. They come and go at will. Sometimes a whole day's journey lies under an overcast sky, at others scarcely a cloud comes across the sun from its rising to its setting.

I would weave my story willingly after this chequered pattern if I could, but it is told in sober earnest, and I must just go on in my own fashion to the end, which is not so far off now.

My father did not know what to make of it when nothing came of what he had said to Hildred, and all went on seemingly much as usual.

According to his custom he asked no questions, only gave sundry vexed impatient looks at the door, and at Martha Clifford, when for several days she came in alone to wait on him. On her part she went about with pursed-up lips and a heavy step, setting things to rights with a sort of fling, meant to show that in some way she felt herself to be ill-used.

'Ah,' she began at last, seeing as she came in, that my father's eyes, as usual, looked beyond her in the hope of seeing Hildred following, 'I see well enough what you are after, neighbour Lisle. But I don't mean to put up with it any longer, that I don't.'

'What'll she be at now?' asked my father, looking up at me.

'Willie knows right well. I told him how it would be if he went on about Cuthbert Franklyn any longer, talking to Hildred and scaring her. There's the girl been crying all night: Phillis heard her. But there'll be an end to it all, for I am going to send her away to her aunt in Morechester. She'll be left in peace there, at all events.'

Martha kept her word. Prayers and promises availed nothing. She sent Hildred to Morechester, to be shut up all through the bright summer in a hot town, in rooms above a shop. Her aunt, a good woman enough I believe, lived in one of those quaint old houses in the market-place, that had a carved wooden gallery running round it, and a high-pitched roof with a gilt weathercock at the top.

They told me Hildred was content to be there. On market days

I used to see her standing in the old-fashioned bow-window, watching the busy scene round the Cross—watching perhaps, I thought, for me. It was the moment in each week I lived for. They would not let me go and see her.

She always had a bright colour, and a smile when I caught sight of her, but even from that distance I could see that she was growing thin.

They left her there for many months, poor child, till long after the summer days were gone. Late in autumn Matt Clifford's heart smote him at her wistful face, as he was bidding her good-bye one day, and he brought her home.

Martha talked and scolded, blamed Hildred for looking ill, Matt for giving in to her when it was not for her real good, and me, for meaning, as of course I did, to begin again doing all I could towards wearing Hildred into her grave.

Clifford—I had never liked him so well—came and spoke to me himself, in a manly, straightforward way, and with a fairness that gave double weight to all his words. Hildred had no one but him and his wife, belonging to her, he said. He stood in her father's place, and wished to do his duty by her the same as if she was one of his own children. If he spoke now it was because he thought that it was right he should, not because he cared to meddle and make; 'as you know well enough, Will,' he added with a half smile, 'seeing how many years I have let things be and have said nothing either way.' 'He was sure,' he went on, 'that I had meant to do rightly by Hildred and Cuthbert both. As far as he could see, I could have done nothing but wait to see if Cuthbert would come home. When a man gave his word, why, he must stick to it. But there was an end to everything: the living ought not to suffer for the dead. To his mind it was time now to think a little more of Hildred. 'For betwixt you both,' said Clifford, looking up again with his grave smile, 'she is getting wasted to a shadow. What with Cuthbert's going away, and never sending a word home, and with your not letting her believe—as they tell me—that Cuthbert is dead and gone, what with all this, there'll be naught left of her soon. I tell you where it is, Will: I want to have her forget; if he's dead, fretting won't bring him back; if so be as he's alive, you'll never make me think he couldn't have sent so much as a line home to his sweetheart in these many years. I don't want to think so badly of him,' said Clifford 'as that he's living still.'

'Did you never think he might have been made prisoner?' I asked.

'I never think anything, but that he was killed, as David Moore told us. Hearing that, you are set free concerning any word you passed to him. That being so, I ask you now what you are going to do.'

I was silent.

'I should have no call to speak,' Clifford went on frankly, 'no call whatsoever, if Hildred had not been told by your father that you had been partial to her yourself, as long ago as before Cuthbert went. Maybe it was no business of his to tell—that I must leave—but as she knows it, for my wife had it from your father himself (Hildred never spoke a word), how can we look for her to settle down, seeing you every day?'

'What is it you would have me do?' I asked.

'I don't want you to marry the girl, mind,' said her brother, with a sort of pride for her in his voice. 'I don't want her to marry anybody, God bless her, unless she likes. As long as I am spared she has a home with me, and welcome. But I should wish to say to her—if so it is to be—that she needn't think any more of either you or him. She's but young yet, and my hope is that she'll turn her mind to some one else, after a bit. Still, I seem to feel vexed for you, Will. You are very fond of her, and I think, though she doesn't say a word, that she's very fond of you. It seems as though it were a pity to waste your two lives just for what I call an idea.'

'Will you give me a little time to think it over?' I asked, more perplexed than I had ever been before.

'To be sure,' he said heartily. 'I don't require you to do aught in haste. But consider that here's Christmas a-coming round again, and it'll be two years come Christmas Day since we heard for certain that Cuthbert was dead. It don't seem likely,' and Matt grew quite warm, 'it don't seem natural that he'd never have sent home a line—being in life—just to say "Don't mourn along o' me, dear friends, for I'm above ground yet." That's how I look at it.'

It is no good telling you all I thought. There has been too much about my thoughts already. I had striven so long to keep the balance even; it needed but a feather-weight to make it tremble now. Clifford's reasoning—Hildred's forced smiles—the thought that it was possible, after all that had come and gone, that she could ever turn her mind to some one else, some happy man who would be free to woo her, and would win her heart at last—these were not feather-weights. The length of time did make some difference too. Cuthbert himself would surely say that I had waited long enough honestly to fulfil his trust. I pondered over my answer to Matt's question for a whole month. At the end the balance was not even any longer.

There was one chance left of my getting good advice, for Master

Caleb Morton was coming to spend the Christmas holidays at Furzy Nook. All my hopes were fixed on asking his counsel. We had not met since the beginning of all my troubles, more than four years ago.

Well, he came, and what was more, his wife and Mrs. Janet came with him. Such a welcome as they got from all Wyncliffe! It was a long while before I could get a quiet time to tell my story.

'There are no two ways about it,' said Mrs. Janet. She was the first to break a long silence, after all was told. She stood, knitting-needles in hand, working vigorously while she talked. 'There are no two ways about it. It is Willie's duty to marry Hildred Clifford. The thing is beyond a doubt. Young Franklyn, we are positively told, is long since dead. Therefore Willie is at liberty, and I say, bound, to marry the girl he loves, and who loves him. That's clear enough.'

'You think so, Janet?' said her brother thoughtfully.

'To be sure I do. The thing is as plain as a pike-staff.'

'I wish I could be as sure of it as you are.'

'Why, it's common sense. Willie will see it himself, and make up his mind, now that it is put before him properly—that is, if he is as sensible as he ought to be after the learning he got from you.'

'But I haven't made up my own mind,' said my dear old master.

'Brother, I am surprised at you. What would you have? You can't keep faith with a dead man, and I'm sure he wouldn't wish it him-self. Cuthbert Franklyn was an open-hearted generous lad, when I remember him, and would have been the last to stand in the way of Willie's welfare. No, Willie's present duty is to make little Hildred Clifford happy, not to keep a fanciful promise that had much better never have been made at all.'

'I protest I think Janet is right,' said Master Caleb. 'I do indeed. The more I think of it the more sensible it seems.'

They went on strengthening each other in the opinion they had formed, while I listened with a beating heart, hearing Mrs. Janet as-sert, and my master agree with her, that it was my bounden duty to set aside the past. The turning of the tide had come at length.

I looked towards Dorothy, sitting somewhat apart beside the fire. She had not spoken, but once or twice had raised her eyes quickly from her work. Latterly she had laid it down on her lap, as if to listen more carefully, and was looking thoughtfully from one to the other as they spoke. Master Caleb followed the direction of my eyes.

'Do you want to know what she thinks?' he said, brightening up.

'If she would be so kind.'

'Dorothy,' he called. She came nearer and laid her hand on his shoulder. 'Willie wants your advice, and your help Dorothy.'

She hesitated a little, and looked at Mrs. Janet, who nodded to her, and said—

'Well, speak up child!'

'But Janet must know so much better than I do,' Dorothy began.

'Bless me!' Mrs. Janet broke in. 'Why, you are not going to say Dorothy, child, that you don't think of it as I do.'

'I thought,' Dorothy began again, and then stopped.

'There can be no two ways about it,' said Mrs. Janet, knitting faster.

'Go on, Dorothy,' said her husband watching her.

'I don't like seeming to set myself up against Janet,' she said, with her frank smile.

'Is that all?' Mrs. Janet patted her shoulder. 'Always know your mind, my dear, and speak it. I am going into the window to turn the heel of my stocking, and I shan't hear you. So say your say, child, and don't think of me—not that there can be two ways about it, all the same, you know.'

Dorothy turned round to me quickly. 'You want to know what I think?'

I said if she pleased I did indeed.

'Then, Willie, remember Cuthbert's trust in you, remember your promise, and help Hildred to keep hers.'

There was a short silence.

'You know there is every reason to believe Cuthbert Franklyn to be dead,' said Master Caleb, in a low voice.

'I know it; we cannot tell. It may be so—God alone knows. That question is in His hands not ours. But is Willie set free from the solemn word he gave? Can he marry Hildred now, and yet feel that he is faithful to the trust he took upon him, and true to the friend who left all he cared for, without a fear, in his keeping? Willie,' she went on, 'it is very hard for you, a long hard trial and a rough path may lie before you. It may be also that in this world you will never see that you were right. Perhaps at the close of your life you will say, "Well, all these years I might have been happy, and only for a doubt I have been lonely all my life." But I think even then you will not grudge the long struggle or the lonely years, and that you will draw near to your end more peacefully, for having tried to do your duty to the uttermost and to be "faithful unto death."'

I bent my head down lower and lower as she spoke. I was ashamed to raise it up. Her words had swept away the mists that had seemed to be rising round me and confusing me. The right was growing clear once more. The bright haze that had dazzled my weak eyes was passing away, and my duty stood stern and plain again before me.

I could not speak, but stood before her with my eyes bent on the ground.

'It was for Hildred's sake he doubted,' said my kind master, almost pleadingly.

'I know it,' she answered very softly. 'I know it was; but Hildred will be glad too, some day, that Willie has guarded her even against herself. He must find strength for her also. It seems to me that there could be for them no true content or rest, for the shadow of a trust betrayed and of a broken word would stand between them, and day by day the cloud of a fear they would not dare to speak of would darken over their lives.'

There was silence all through the room. No one answered. My master still sat half-turned and looking up at her. Mrs. Janet had left the window and was facing us. Her hands were held in the attitude of knitting, but the needles did not move, nor did she try to speak. I saw them all without knowing that I looked. At last Mistress Dorothy spoke again.

'Willie,' she said—the colour had flushed into her face, and its earnestness made her beautiful to look at—'Willie, not to every one is granted the opportunity of a great self-sacrifice. If God has willed that your path should be very difficult, do not be afraid to walk in it, for He will surely help you. Do not think so much of what you *may* do, as of what you *can* do—of what you can give up at His call. Choose the highest, for it will lead you nearer to Him. I am a weak woman. I know I should not be strong enough to walk in your hard path; but Willie'—she came near to me and took my hand,—'hitherto you have been so noble and so true. Brave heart, be faithful to the end.'

The kind words, so unlooked for, so undeserved, came too suddenly upon me. I had so nearly failed, and she said this. I kissed her hand—

When I looked up again, the tears were raining down her face, Master Caleb's eyes were shaded by his hand, and Mrs. Janet was in the window, standing with her back to us.

* * * *

They say that to every cloud there is a silver lining. I was very sure that there were clouds on my horizon, but not quite so certain about the silver lining. If there was one at all, it must have been Jock

Clifford.

For when you are in trouble there is a great deal of comfort to be got out of a child's affection.

In those days, after Matt Clifford had received my answer to his question in cold silence—when Martha would not let Hildred go near our house, and had forbidden her, as nearly as she could, to speak to me—when my father never opened his lips but to complain of me, I fell back with a singular feeling of refreshment and consolation, on my one staunch friend Jock.

He had been my shadow ever since, some nine or ten years ago, he began to stand alone on his sturdy little legs. Robin and Walter, his twin elder brothers, had no time to notice him. They were absorbed in a never-ending struggle, which of them should have the upper hand—a struggle that had begun as long ago as when, two red-faced babies, they lay heads and tails in the same cradle. It never seemed likely to be settled in their life-time, and it made them very quarrelsome, and quite inseparable.

So Jock, left to himself, bestowed all his company upon me. When one is in disgrace with well nigh all the world—and very few people made up 'all the world' to me,—it is at all events something to have a friend left, in whose eyes the idea of your doing anything wrong is a matter of simple impossibility—it is something, even though the friend be only eleven years old.

Jock was no half-hearted champion. He had found that he could make his mother pinch up her lips and raise her eyebrows, merely by praising me. So he talked of me incessantly, partly for love of me, and partly to use this his newly-gotten power. He was somewhat pleased too, only half offended, at Aunt Hildred frequently giving him kisses and lumps of barley sugar, behind the door.

Knowing that I was not very welcome to any one else, I fell, in my down-heartedness, rather an easy prey to Jock's overflowing life and glee, and he led me hither and thither, that spring, pretty nearly as he would. Neither work nor play came amiss to him. Ratting, rook-shooting and rabbit-snaring Jock's soul delighted in—most of all, perhaps, helping me to fish the trout stream that ran under the Castle walls.

No wonder he liked it. My own troubles seemed to fade away, as I laid the line lightly across the stream. Ah, those spring days, when the 'March brown' was on the water, how fair they were! A bluff wind came singing up the valley, crisping the clear brown water and crowning each little wave with silver ripples; a soft pearly sky, with now and then a dash of pale spring sunshine that lighted up woods and stream, and showed how the red buds were bursting into leaf, and a tender shining green, was beginning to clothe the alder trees.

My eyes, and Jock's, were fastened on to the water. I felt, rather than saw, that spring's soft fingers were at work along the banks; that a tuft of starry primroses had been nestled into the mossy root of an old willow, and a yellow butterfly, the first of the year, hung fluttering over them. Farther on a whole bed of violets, purple and white, glittered, fragrance-breathing, on the bank. The wind swept through the boughs merrily, trying in play to tear off the new leaves; but the stout little things held fast and laughed back, as they were swayed up and down. The whole bright summer was theirs to flutter through, before the wind could claim them as his own; and the birds and the wind and the sunshine spoke with their hundred tongues, and said, 'Ah, poor mortals! you may fret, and dispute, and sorrow as you will; you cannot keep back the summer. It is coming. It is coming.'

One day that spring I was bidden to a wedding at the Ferry-house; and I went, rejoicing heartily for both bride and bridegroom's sake. If ever I saw a face that beamed with contentment it was the bridegroom's.

Patience—his best helper—had won the day for him, and Elfrida wedded her faithful suitor at last.

For David Moore had come home for good, cured of his love of wandering and fighting, and well pleased to settle down for the rest of his days at the ferry.

The old people Elfrida had worked for so long wanted her no more. Davy—well, if it be true that clouds have silver linings it is not less so that each rose has its thorn. I thought of that on the wedding day, when the moment came for Elfrida to part with Davy. She was as quiet as usual until then, waiting upon everybody, and looking as if nothing had happened. But when the horse with the pillion on it, stood ready to carry her 'home,' Elfrida's heart gave way. She knelt on the ground, hugging Davy to her, kissing his curls, his frock, his little restless hands. Her husband stood waiting for her, compassionate and a little impatient. Davy himself had one arm round her neck, but his eyes were wandering to the horse, and he was eager to see Elfrida ride away. 'Oh Baby,' she sobbed, going back in her distress to the first name she had loved him by; 'Won't Baby kiss poor Frida?'

Davy looked at her, wondering. He had never seen her cry before. He put the other arm round her neck and kissed her gravely on each cheek. Immediately afterwards he gave her up as a bad job, being quite unable to fathom such a depth of grief as two kisses from him were not sufficient to cure.

That would be the way with him all his days. He was made, in his careless beauty, to win hearts without trying, to be loved and worshipped and wept over. There would always be plenty of Elfridas thankful to work for him in the shadow, while he walked through life in the sunshine.

But now her willing slavery was ending. The last words were spoken. The old shoe was thrown after her for luck. The setting sun was turning the river—her old comrade—into a sheet of gold.

Elfrida rode away up into the hills behind her goodman, and the ferry-boat knew her no more.

'Life,' said Martha Clifford musingly, 'is a muddle. Births and deaths—comings and goings—weddings and funerals—the young marry and the old die; that's the way of the world.'

She was standing by my father's bedside as she reflected thus. Elfrida's was the wedding that was just past; my father's the death that it seemed would follow hard upon it.

He had been failing all the winter; but now we counted his remaining life by days, nay, it might be, by hours. Martha had softened towards me since he was 'taken,' as she called it, 'for death.' Both she and Hildred helped to tend him.

And it came about that, before my father died, even the cause of difference that had been between us was taken away.

It was but natural that they should blame me for still clinging to such a mere shadow as the hope that Cuthbert might be alive. But I thought that it must be God Himself who kept alight in my heart the little spark of faith that no one shared, and that would not be extinguished. Now I know that it was so.

For I was right after all. At last—at last, he came. One evening, after Martha and Hildred had gone home and I was alone downstairs, I heard the latch move as if some one was trying to lift it with an unsteady hand. Then the door opened, and the sunshine and the shadow fell across the floor—a man's shadow. I looked round carelessly, for I was not thinking of him then. Other cares—my father's illness and Hildred's presence, had driven him lately out of my mind. He had not been so far from my thoughts for years as lately, when day by day he was coming nearer to me.

Now, as I was telling you, I saw a shadow cast from the doorway. I turned round. There, on the threshold stood a soldier in a worn greatcoat—a dark man, with the empty sleeve of his right arm fastened across his breast. As I got up, he took off his hat and spoke my name.

How did we meet? I cannot tell. What words does one use after such a parting? How can you greet one, come back, as it were, through the grave and gate of death? I only remember hearing myself say over and over again, 'Cuthbert, Cuthbert.'

'You thought that I was dead.' His voice deep and grave, was as the voice of a stranger.

'Never; I could not believe it; others might, I never did.'

'Faithful old Willie.' He smiled, and then it was Cuthbert again.

I wanted to push him down into the arm-chair in the chimney-corner, and tried to welcome him in such broken words as I could find.

Was it very strange that, in the quick rush of joy at seeing his face once more, I forgot Hildred for a moment—forgot all but that my brother had come home? His next words brought all back. He put his hand on my shoulder and said 'Hildred?' and I felt his grasp tighten as if he tried to steady himself.

'She is at home, and well.'

He drew a long breath without speaking, and my words too were checked.

'I am going to her,' he said next.

'Oh Cuthbert, stop—remember. She knows nothing, she has long given you up. It will kill her if you come upon her suddenly.'

Cuthbert pushed away my hand with a smile. 'Joy does not kill,' he said.

Joy! I do not know which I thought of at that moment, joy or sorrow, Cuthbert or Hildred, the sudden shock of their meeting to her, or the blow it might bring to him.

'Let me go to her first,' I said eagerly: 'let me tell her.' I do not know what I meant to do. I think I had some wild idea of imploring her to love him.

Cuthbert looked surprised. 'No, no,' he said, 'I want to see her first glad look. Don't keep me.'

I suppose in my perturbation I was going to follow him, for he stopped and said, 'Let me go alone, Will. Dear old fellow, I don't want even you when I first see my Hildred.'

I let him go—let him go to her whom he called his own. He was right—his, not mine. And I had been so madly glad to see him!

Cuthbert was not gone for very long. He came in slowly, came up to me, and—he had not done it since we were little boys together—bent down and kissed me. My heart was beating hard and fast.

'You have seen her?'

'Yes'—he sank down wearily into a chair—'I have seen her.'

'Well?'

'Well'—he looked up and smiled rather sadly—'Well, the joy did not kill her, you see.'

'She was glad?'

'I hope so. I hope so indeed.'

'What then, Cuthbert? Did she know you?'

He leant down his head on the table, and suddenly burst into tears. My whole heart went back to him.

'Cuthbert—what is it?'

He spoke almost directly. 'I am a worn-out old soldier. I have lost my arm. I am good for nothing now, and I think she was disappointed in me.'

Oh Cuthbert, whom in my heart I had almost hated just now—true soldier, faithful heart—to see his brave head bent low. He should be happy whatever became of me.

I told him to be comforted, that all would be well, and by-and-by he began to believe what he so much wished. 'I have looked forward to this for so long,' he said. 'I have had so much hardship and suffering. For two years we were in an Indian prison, and I should not have cared to live, only for the thought that Hildred would grieve for me. And now to see her so changed, so white and strange.'

'You frightened her, poor child. Remember that she had long given up the hope of seeing you again.'

'You had not.'

'Ah, Cuthbert, that was so different.'

He gave a long sigh. 'Perhaps I had better not have come back at all. I had better not have lived.'

'But you must live now, for your little Hildred's sake.' I could say it with no sharp pang at my heart. A great peacefulness came over me, like the evening air after a storm. That night, as I sat up alone beside my father's bed, I prayed for Cuthbert and Hildred. For myself I only needed to thank God for His mercy to me.

It was scarcely light the next morning when Jock's low whistle under the window called me out to him. Hildred had sent him, he said, to tell me to go and speak to her. She was in the chapel, waiting for me.

Day had not long broken outside. Inside the ruined aisle of the chapel was full of shadows still, but through the great window facing the east we could see the dawn brighten and grow strong. Hildred had chosen a strange place of meeting. Here all told how earthly joy and earthly sorrow vanish and pass away. Beneath our feet, as we trod the broken pavement, were the graves of men whose hopes and fears had long been over; their very names were worn away by the footsteps of later generations. Deep and unbroken seemed the repose of the happy dead. What matter now to them how heavy the cross had been, so that they had won the crown? What matter how hard and long the battle had been once, so that they had been faithful unto death? A thrill of awe crossed me as I looked up the solemn aisle in the grey morning light. There too the sculptured angel that in my childhood I used to call my mother, looked down gravely with outstretched wings, as if she were watching over her son in this the crisis of his life.

Hildred was there, leaning against an old carved tomb. She was quite white, and her eyes had a scared and weary look as she raised them to me.

I am afraid that I spoke the more sternly, for the love I felt for her, the great longing I had to take her to my heart and comfort her.

'Well, Hildred,' I said, gravely, 'you sent for me.'

'I was so frightened,' she whispered. 'Oh Willie, tell me what I ought to do.'

'Your duty.'

Just as she used to do when she was a child, she covered her face and shrank down on to the ground.

'But it is so hard to do one's duty—so hard.'

'Oh child,' I answered, from my heart, 'it is hard, but God is good.'

Then I tried to plead Cuthbert's cause, and to tell her how the remembrance of her had been the one thing he clung to through his dark days of imprisonment and pain—the one thing, failing which he would have been glad, for very weariness, to lie down and die.

'If we have failed him—you and I—in these years that he has trusted us—and in my heart I know that I have failed in deed, if not in will—oh Hildred, it is not too late yet. We have time, and Cuthbert trusts us still.'

'You never think of anyone but Cuthbert,' said Hildred, impatiently, unknowing how cruel her words sounded.

'I think of you too, Hildred,' I answered, very sadly. 'I am very sorry for you both.'

'Would Cuthbert mind so very much,' asked Hildred, 'if he knew how long it was before we gave him up?'

'You will never tell him you forgot him,' I said, in terror.

She was silent.

'God help him, then. God help us all.'

Neither of us spoke for many minutes—slow minutes that were

laden with heavy thoughts.

At last Hildred looked up to me with a smile that was wonderfully sweet and sad.

'Willie,' she said, 'I wish I could be as strong as you are.'

'You can, Hildred. Oh dear Hildred, you will be if you try.'

'Oh, I am going to try, of course,' she answered, wearily.

Cuthbert was standing before the door when I went home. We shook hands and went into the house together, but I had a strange feeling all the time, that I did not know what to say to him. Last night I fancied that my battle was all over, and the victory mine once and for ever. This morning it all began over again, and every word that Cuthbert spoke ruffled me. I felt angry with him for speaking cheerily, and gave all my attention to lighting the fire. He stood leaning his arm on the chimney-piece, and watching me.

'It seems odd to see you doing all the woman's work,' he said.

I answered shortly that there was no one else to do it.

'So dear old Granny is gone?'

'Yes, long ago.'

'How long?'

'Oh, two years and more.'

'Dear, kind old Granny. She was very good to me.'

I said nothing.

'Do you think your father is getting better?' he asked presently.

'No, I don't. He never will be better.'

Cuthbert looked down at me in his old kind way.

'Poor old Will, you have had troubles even here at home.'

'Yes, one doesn't need to go to the wars for that,' I answered.

'And yet I fancied you all so happy here, except that I thought Hildred must fret about me at times. Did she, Will?'

'Of course. Everybody was uneasy about you.'

And then I was glad to get away to my father's room. But when I came down Cuthbert would talk of Hildred, and ask questions about her. He seemed to have forgotten the fears he had last night. She had been startled, he said, but it would be all right to-day. And by-and-by he went away to seek her.

The day passed slowly and heavily. My father lay with his eyes half closed, scarcely noticing anything. I did not let Cuthbert see him, for fear of disturbing him, but later in the day, when Hildred and Martha were with him, he heard the strange footstep on the stairs. Cuthbert's step now, soldierly and measured, was very unlike the light quick tread my father used to know. It was no remembrance that made him turn his head on the pillow to listen, and then say to

Hildred, 'Who?'

I tried to turn his attention away, but the footstep crossed the room below, and my father repeated, 'Who is it?'

'Cuthbert Franklyn,' Hildred said, quietly.

'Cuthbert!' There was very little surprise in his voice as he repeated the name. 'Cuthbert! Bring him here.'

I went outside the room and called him. I was sorry my father should find out that Cuthbert was there, but I saw in a few minutes that it mattered very little. The small interests of Time, its lights and shadows, were growing faint and dim for the eyes on which Eternity was just about to dawn.

My father held out his hand feebly when Cuthbert stood beside his bed. After a minute he looked up at him again, and murmured a few words, too low for any of us to catch distinctly. I believe they were something about fishing, and that his thoughts were wandering back to when Cuthbert was a boy. He did not need an answer. In a few minutes he was lying quietly as before.

Cuthbert stood for a while at the foot of the bed and then went away.

It made me feel more than ever that I was alone. My father had cared so much about my marrying Hildred; and now Cuthbert's return, which put an end to that thought for ever, awoke no interest in him. He was neither surprised nor sorry that Cuthbert and Hildred should have been standing together beside his bed.

Hildred was very quiet. She waited on my father with careful tenderness, and avoided as much as she could speaking to me. When she had done everything for my father, she stood still for a long while looking down at him. Perhaps, like me, she half-envied him his peaceful rest.

Nearly everybody in the village came up in the course of the day to see Cuthbert. The news of his return had spread far and wide, and his old friends thronged to welcome him, hardly able to believe that he was really the Cuthbert Franklyn they had so long talked of as dead. Everybody wished me joy.

'I'm sure I'm as glad as though it had been a son of my own,' said good old Esther Reynolds. 'I knew how you'd feel, Willie, let alone Hildred. Just at this time too, it seems sent to cheer you up a bit, now your father lies so ill. I said so when I heard the news, and that I must make shift to get up to the Castle and tell Willie Lisle how I thought about him; for, as I said to my master, the two boys were wonderful fond of each other—more than most real brothers. Now there are my two lads, quarrelled at the fair last Michaelmas, and haven't so much as spoken one to the t'other since.'

Cuthbert looked at me and I at him, and we held out our hands to each other. Everybody was shaking hands and we were not noticed. As I felt his strong left-handed grasp, something that was like a cloud seemed to roll away from between us.

'It's all right now, old chap,' he said, low enough for no one but me to hear.

So it was 'all right' from that time forth between him and me. But he began by degrees to see that Hildred was changed, and that his fancy the night he had come home was no mistake.

He was very patient and gentle to her, even when she was the most changeable or cold. He never complained; only he often sat still without speaking, with a sad look on his face.

'I must give her time,' he said to me once or twice. 'It will come right by-and-by. I have grown strange to her. Will, I sometimes think this is a judgment on me for the selfish way I went and left her when I first enlisted.'

'You must wait,' I used to say.

'Oh yes, I will; I am trying to be very patient, and I believe that she will come back to me in time.'

I don't think he ever really doubted that. His trust in her, like his love for her, was perfect.

My father's state was reason enough for settling nothing. We all felt it to be a time of waiting. For myself, I looked forward very little. A merciful kind of lull and calmness had come across my life, as I watched over my father's last days.

He died as silently as he had lived. I had wished for some spoken word to tell me he was happy, and that the hand of the Good Shepherd was guiding him through the valley of the shadow of death. But it was not so to be. An upward look; a clasping of the hands; a deep 'Amen,' uttered at the end of the prayers the vicar offered by his bed; a smile when the most comforting of all names was spoken to him. Those were the outward signs he gave.

For the rest, who can tell what was passing in his mind during those silent nights and days?

The end came towards morning, after a night of storm and rain. The wind was shaking the lattice windows and moaning round the ruins. We were all gathered about his bed—Cuthbert and I, Matt Clifford and his wife, and Hildred. When, towards midnight, the strange change that even those who have seen little of death know instinctively, began to come across his face Cuthbert went to fetch them. Everyone was quite quiet except poor Hildred. She could not keep back her sobs, as she knelt with her face hidden on the side of the bed.

I saw Cuthbert move round, and without speaking put his hand on her bowed head.

All seemed unreal and far away to me, except my father's over-shadowed face and deep-drawn breath. 'He does not know anything,' said Martha Clifford, watching him.

But as if he somehow felt the coming of the morning, he stirred and opened his eyes, and in a thick indistinct voice he asked the hour.

I bent over and told him.

The next moment he said, 'Is it day-break?'

No, it was still quite dark; but a new, bright unearthly smile came over his face. With a thrill of awe and wonder we looked to see it fade——

'It is over,' Martha Clifford said.

And the smile remained.

* * * *

A few days more, and the slow tolling of the church bell called us to go down and lay our dead under the shadow of the grey belfry.

My father's burial was over, and we had come back to the empty house. All that afternoon I sat by the fire-place in his vacant chair, and tried to think of what I ought to do.

The house was quite silent, and the door, as usual in summer, stood half open.

Somehow I fell to thinking of my mother more than of my father. It was just on such a quiet afternoon as this that I came home years ago, after she was dead, and found Cuthbert near the well. I thought of the message Master Caleb brought me from her, bidding me be as a brother to Cuthbert, and I wondered whether she would still have sent it, if she could have known all that was to follow. What would she have had me do now? The way did not seem clear before me. All my kith and kin were gone. I had seen them carried one by one across the threshold, and had stood by while they were laid to rest in the churchyard down yonder. Mother first; then the kind old grand-mother, and now my father. I was as much alone as Cuthbert was when he first came to us. The wheel of life had turned round since then, and left me poor.

Cuthbert stayed with me for some time, sitting in the chair op-posite to mine, and trying every now and then, poor fellow, to find something cheering to say to me. But I did not care to talk, so at last he went to the door and let in more sunshine as he pushed it open; then he came back to me, and after putting his hand on my shoulder and saying something about going to look for Hildred he went away.

I was glad to be left alone, though Cuthbert was grave and sad enough, and almost as ready to sit silently thinking as I was. He and my father had never been much to each other. Yet it was the breaking of a long tie, and the losing of the last bit of the old life. Besides, he was unhappy about Hildred.

I suppose a long time passed while I still sat thinking, for the sun came round to the other window, and cast long level rays into the room.

Suddenly a great noise roused me—a loud crash and then a rumbling sound, as if loose stones were falling over one another. Once before I had heard something like it when a part of the Castle wall had fallen. I went out quickly now, towards the part of the ruin that the sound came from.

Hildred met me as I passed under the arch near the keep. She was as pale as death. She clutched my arm and tried to speak. I could barely hear what she said, for some horror seemed to be choking her, and she gasped for breath. She pulled me back in the direction from which she came.

'I have killed him. Come!'

'Hildred what is it? Where is Cuthbert?'

She pointed across the ruins. Still in the same hoarse whisper she said, 'The tower fell in; I took him there.'

It was true; part of the tower had fallen. It was the oldest bit of the ruin, and the walls were mouldering away. I had often warned Hildred that it was unsafe. Now I saw a great heap of massive fallen stones and masonry, and a huge gap in the wall. A bit of the winding stone stair was down. Far above our heads the broken steps began again. Merciful Heaven! was Cuthbert buried under all that?

'Can he be alive?' Hildred gasped, and ended with a long wild scream, as she saw the horror in my face.

'Hush, Hildred, I must get the tools; call Matt; send the boys for help.'

When I came back Matt Clifford was there. Hildred had flung herself down upon the fallen stones and was tearing at the rough masses with her bare hands.

Poor child! I must tell you now, what I heard afterwards, why she said that she had done it. I did not ask then, only worked for dear life, and spoke no words, except a few which I will tell you later.

Cuthbert had found her when he left me. She was thinking of my father, and her heart, she said, was full of longing to come and comfort me in my trouble. 'It seemed hardest of all not to be able to tell you how sorry I was. Your father was always so good to me.'

So when Cuthbert joined her she was cross with him, and reproached him for having left me alone at such a time. He was very gentle and patient, but she would not listen. They wandered on as they talked, and came to this tower. Hildred wanted to get away from him, and began to climb the winding stair, bidding him not follow her. Half way up there was a broken window, out of which we often used to jump as children, on to the wall beneath. She reached this in safety, but Cuthbert had come after her; turning round she saw the stair waver beneath his greater weight. The wall rocked to and fro—bent inwards—and then came the awful crash which I had heard, and Cuthbert was gone.

I knew it was useless, yet I could not help bending down and calling out his name. No answer. A dead silence there, but behind, the welcome sound of hurrying steps, as man after man came up to us, breathless, horror-stricken, eager to help.

We fell to work, working as men only can when life or death seems hanging on their hands. Scarcely a word was uttered. There was only the sound of the pickaxes driven deep down into the heaps of rubbish,—the grating noise of stones raised up and thrown aside—by-and-by the quickened breathing of those who would not stop to rest. On and on, with a grim energy, and agony of suspense, that seemed to double the power in those strong arms and quivering muscles. On and on, with wild words of voiceless prayer ringing in my ears, with thoughts that wandered strangely to my father's funeral, to the tolling of the church bell, to Hildred standing sobbing by the open grave.

She was close beside me. Her hands were torn and bleeding, cut by the sharp stones which she was trying madly to lift up and roll away. The gravel that the spades threw aside, fell all over her, but she did not know it. I lifted her up, for there was not room enough for all the workers, who could give stronger help than hers. She struggled to get away from me, telling me to let her go back and help.

'You cannot help us so,' I said. 'Hildred! poor child, kneel down and pray for us.'

'Oh, I cannot. I do not know how. I am too wicked. Tell me what to say.'

Somehow, the solemn words that we had heard that day, standing by my father's grave, came to my lips, and I repeated them.

'In the midst of life we are in death. Of whom may we seek for succour but of Thee, O Lord, who for our sins art justly displeased?'

Hildred had fallen on her knees, repeating 'Oh, justly displeased, most justly.'

I was back at work. I heard Hildred say, 'Won't some one pray again?' and presently an old man, the parish clerk, standing near her, said in a broken voice, with many pauses, 'In all time of our tribulation, in the hour of death, and in the day of judgment——'

From us all—from poor Hildred—from the eager workers, and the watchers standing by, came as with one voice, the deep response, 'Good Lord, deliver us.'

The time was drawing near when we should know the worst. The great heap of fallen masonry was getting smaller every minute. Could Cuthbert have been saved alive? We came upon great stems of ivy crushed and broken in the ruin. The fresh leaves, unwithered yet, shone out strangely here and there.

Hildred had not moved. She was kneeling, almost lying on the ground. The setting sun was shining in our eyes, dazzling us as we worked, with what seemed to me—calm, pitiless curiosity.

A great stone, almost the last, was lifted on one side. From those in front there suddenly rose a sort of cheer, checked instantly, a smothered exclamation, and then an eager silence, as they bent over something on the ground.

I gave one look, went back to Hildred, and knelt down by her. I burst out crying like a child when I began to speak. I could not help it. Then I took her hand and told her, 'Hildred, dear heart, be comforted. There is hope.'

He was not crushed. God had guarded him. He had fallen in some manner sheltered from the great stones, by the wall and the remains of the staircase. He was half buried under the bits of broken wall, and he lay quite still and unconscious at our feet. But he might be living yet. We carried him out, and laid him down in the sunshine.

Was it life or death—that rigid figure that did not move, that ashen-grey face, with the thin stream of blood trickling from the temple?

Hildred was on the ground beside him, gazing into his face with straining eyes, that seemed as if they must call him back from death itself. She lifted up his arm and tried to put it round her. She called to him, first in a choked whisper, then louder, yet louder, as his silence struck the chill of terror more into her heart.

'Cuthbert, Cuthbert! Oh come back! Forgive me! Dear Cuthbert, speak to me!'

The men stood round watching her. I heard some of them crying, great rough fellows as they were. Hildred looked up at me with bright, widely-opened eyes—no tears in them. Then she spoke to him again, called on him to come back, and she would love him. He heard her. Some tone of hers must have reached him even then. He moved, drew a faint sigh. Oh the low cry she gave! It was not a word or a sob, but just the half-stifled first cry of a new-born hope.

And then Cuthbert opened his eyes, saw her leaning over him, and smiled. She did not speak, only bent down lower, until her face lay hidden by her hands upon his breast.

In a few minutes, very slowly and feebly he raised his hand and put it on her head.

Cuthbert was taken to Clifford's house, which was much nearer at hand than ours. For a few hours more we watched him anxiously. Life came back slowly, but at length the doctor turned away from the bed with a sigh of relief. 'He will do now,' he said cheerily. 'Only keep him quiet. Why, it would never have done to let him slip through our fingers in this sort of way, after his getting over his wounds and escaping out of that Indian prison, as they tell me he did.'

By the next day he could speak to us in a weak voice, and had revived enough to smile a little when Martha told him he had got no more than he deserved, for mooning about in places where Jock himself knew better than to venture.

Towards evening I left him comfortably asleep. Hildred followed me out of the porch, and closed the house door behind her. For a few minutes we did not speak, but stood looking at the setting sun, and thinking—at least I thought—with what different eyes we had seen it going down yesterday, not less peacefully than to-day.

Hildred spoke first, lifting her eyes to mine with a grave rested look that it was new to me to see upon her face.

'God has been merciful,' she said.

'Most merciful.'

'And now——'

My heart was beating fast and heavily. In her grief, in her great terror and her self-reproach, she had seemed to grow dearer to me than ever before; and now that the moment had come—I knew it had—when I must really give her up, I felt as if I could not part with her.

'And now, Willie, I must try to be good at last.' She stopped for a moment, and clasped her hands. 'In that most dreadful time last night, when you told me to pray—when you and the men were working, and I did not know whether or not I had killed him, I made a promise, a solemn promise before God. You know what it was.'

I nodded.

'God gave me back Cuthbert's life. I must try to make it a happy life. I must redeem my promise. Willie, you will help me?'

And so the battle—the hard struggle—was over for her. Well, it was far better so. She was not strong, my darling; she could not have borne a long battle such as a man must fight, so God led her by a short sharp road back to peace.

For a short time we stood together still. Then Hildred turned slowly. 'And now, Willie, just once before I go, I want you to say God bless you.'

As she stood before me looking up at me, I put my hand upon her head, and said, as steadily as I could, 'God bless my dear love for ever, and make her happy.'

The tears were streaming down her face, not bitter tears, but quietly sorrowful. And as I ended she clasped her dear arms for a moment lightly round my neck, and kissed me. That was our farewell. We said no more, and Hildred went away. I watched her until the door closed behind her. When she shut it, the Hildred I loved and who loved me, had passed away from my sight and from my life.

I do not mean that I did not see her, for she was often there when I went to Cuthbert, and after a few days she came with him to the Gatehouse.

Those days, the first of a good many that I had spent quite alone, gave me time to think over many things. My duty began to grow plain to me. Hildred had asked me to help her. I was growing to see more clearly how I could best do so.

Cuthbert got better very quickly. He too, I believe, was thinking a great deal just then of what his future life should be. Hitherto he had been too sad and anxious to make plans, but now that Hildred seemed to have come back to him, he began to wonder how they were to live. He told me so once, when I was sitting by his bed, saying that he would not let it trouble him just yet, he was too happy. Still, he could not help remembering that his pension was very small, and that he had not got two arms like other people. 'I wonder if I can earn enough for Hildred with one arm,' he said. 'Do advise me, Will.'

I asked him to let the future rest for a little longer, and he was content to do so, being weak still, as well as very happy.

In a few days he could walk about again, and one evening he and

Hildred came across the ruins and sat down to rest on the old stone bench outside our house. I remember every little thing that happened on that evening, so like, and yet so unlike, any other that I have ever spent. I could almost repeat each word that was said, every-day and purposeless as some of them would have appeared to any one but me.

I felt as if they must guess my secret, when I asked Cuthbert to come home to-morrow and to look after the house and the Castle gate, while I was away.

'Going away!' said Hildred, looking up.

I was obliged to go to Morechester, I told them, to see the man of business who managed everything about the Castle. He must be told of my father's death, and would settle who was to come after him. Long ago it had been promised that I should do so.

'So it's sure to be all right,' said Cuthbert.

'Oh yes, all right.'

Cuthbert was the one of us who talked the most. He went on to say how like old times it was, for us three to be there together. Neither Hildred nor I made much answer, and presently, following the train of his own thoughts, he began to tell us about his soldier life, his last battle, the dreary years of his imprisonment, and then his escape.

I was glad, and so I think was Hildred, to sit silent and hear him talk. I can see her now, listening quietly and gravely, with her hands folded on her lap. I like to remember her in my mother's place. Often since, I have fancied her sitting there.

The twilight drew on. Now and then a bee, heavily laden, went droning past. The sound of the river rippling over the stones below came to us more clearly. One star shone out. We had been sitting without talking for some time, and Hildred said they must go home.

'I shall be gone before you are awake in the morning,' I said. 'I will leave the key for you.'

They bade me good-night, and went away together.

Cuthbert turned, I have often wondered why, after he had gone a few steps, and came back to wring my hand again. 'Good-night, Will,' he repeated. 'I'll take good care of the old place while you're away. Good speed to you on your journey.'

The words sounded to me like a farewell. 'Will you promise to stay until I come back?' I said, still holding his hand. And he answered, laughing, 'Of course.'

I watched them crossing the Castle Court. Cuthbert was leaning on Hildred. She walked slowly and carefully. Once or twice he bent his head down to talk to her, and I saw her look up to answer him. As they went on she put her hand up to his, which was on her shoulder, as if she told him to lean on her more heavily.

So I lost sight of them in the twilight. God bless them both! It was many years before I saw either of them again.

Later at night, when the moon was up, I went all over the ruins. The grey towers were whitened by the moon-beams, and draped in black ivy, with here and there a silver leaf that the light had fallen upon. From the deep shadow cast by the walls and towers, I passed into the full stream of colourless radiance, then back again into darkness.

For many minutes I stood under Hildred's window, against the diamond-shaped panes of which the moon was glittering. 'Sleep peacefully dear love,' I said to her in my heart. 'Wake happily. God give you bright dreams and gladsome days for ever.'

Lastly, I came to the well, and leaning over the edge looked down wearily. There was the reflection of one sparkling star down there, that lay quivering on the black water. I cannot tell how long I stayed thus; for then I began to lose myself.

The rest of that night, the morrow, and many of the days that followed, are almost a blank in my memory—a blank from which some few pictures stand out more or less distinctly.

I see myself standing before sunrise on the bridge, and turning to take a long last look at the old home. A dewy misty morning had come after the moonlight night. By-and-by it would brighten into a cloudless summer's day; but now the mist hung in heavy folds over the Castle. For an instant the morning breeze might blow it aside and show a glimpse of ruined wall and towered gateway, but the next the white curtain floated back again, and all was hidden.

In the strange confusion that was coming over my thoughts it seemed to me as if those fleecy wreaths of mist were rolling over my whole life, and covering up the past from me for ever.

Next I see Morechester, with burning sunlight blazing on the market-place, and church bells sending abroad their golden waves of sound. Suddenly the glare is quenched as I pass under the arched doorway into the Minster. The air strikes chill, there is a great dimness and silence. From the other end of the nave come echoes as of closing gates and distant footsteps, and presently voices are singing. There is an iron gate which I try to open, but it is locked, and red light shines through a curtain. I am shut out. Within there is peace, and prayer, and sweet music rising up to heaven. Outside I kneel alone by the closed gate. Everything is unreal. I feel as though it were the gate of Paradise that is shut against me. But I can catch that in there they are asking the good Lord to comfort and help the weak-hearted, and the sweet pitying voices that sound as if angels were singing, echo the prayer. They, too, are pleading for me, and I am comforted. And the prayers and the music go their way, and seem to carry me up with them towards heaven.

Again I am in a small dark room, and a grave man is listening while I tell a story. He answers me, and I know that I have won my suit. Cuthbert is to have the Gatehouse instead of me. It is promised to him, and a great load is taken off my mind. Now Cuthbert need fear no future for Hildred or himself. There was but that one way to help them both.

It only remained to send the letter I had already written back to Cuthbert.

It was a good thing that it had been written slowly and carefully beforehand, for now I could not hold my thoughts together, or keep them on one thing for many minutes. In the letter I had told Cuthbert the truth, though not the whole truth. I said that I had grown restless of late, and Wyncliffe had become wearisome to me, so I had gone forth into the world to seek my fortune; and that, if I left them all without saying good-bye they must forgive me—leave-takings were but dreary things; and I knew well how in their kindness they would try to keep me back if they heard that I was going. The rest was easy to say. Cuthbert must know how much rather I would think of him in the old place than of a stranger. He would believe that he was doing me a kindness in filling the post I had given up, so that the life-long tie that bound me to Wyncliffe would be still unbroken, and some one would live in the Gatehouse who loved it as much as I always should, though I was leaving it. I hoped that he and Hildred would be happy there, as we had been long ago.

Then I remember, but very dimly and confusedly, long days of travel, one after the other, during which the only thing I cared for was to get on quickly, farther yet farther, so as to put the greatest distance between myself and all the places I had ever seen.

After that an unknown room; strange, but kindly faces bending over a bed on which I lay, my own voice repeating always, 'Hildred—Cuthbert—little Jock, good-bye,' until my brain seemed to turn round with the weary words.

The thread of memory breaks there.

I find myself again, crossing a moor on an autumn evening. The heather is in bloom still, and looks purple-red in the low rays of the sun. The wide heath, rising and falling like the waves of the sea, stretches on to join the sky. Poised high aloft, on quivering wings, a sky-lark sings its cloud-song. And far away, backed by the golden sunset, there rises the spire of a little church, with a village clustering round it. I am bound there. There is a pack on my shoulders, for I am a pedlar, and am beginning to get the name you have all called me by for so many years. I am Wandering Willie. In those days I had little heart to care what I became. My life seemed to be over. I little thought how long it would yet last.

But it has not been a sad one, though its story, such as it is, ended on the day when I looked my last on the mist-covered towers of Wyncliffe.

The sharp edge of sorrow wears down with time. Peace, the evergreen, grows where joy once blossomed. The road-side flowers bloom fresh and fair, though the garden has been left behind. I would not have things otherwise than as they are. I would not have my youth back, though all I once longed for so passionately were granted with it.

Youth can rarely say I am content, as I can. Young limbs must breast the mountain side, and I have gained the top.

Hildred and Cuthbert lived long and happily. It was some years before I let Cuthbert know where I was. Then immediately he came to me. After that we saw each other every now and then; and though meeting seldom, we were yet friends and brothers, as we had always been. There never was another secret between us. Hildred long before had told her husband all the story of his four years of absence.

But I never went back to Wyncliffe until I was an old man.

It was after an illness that I had, during which my thoughts turned constantly to Hildred. A longing for her presence, that had been stilled for many years, woke up once more and drew me towards her.

When next Cuthbert came to see me I went back with him to Wyncliffe. As in a dream, nay rather, as one returning from the dead, I saw again the once familiar places—the grey church, the lime-trees, the village-green, where they were playing cricket just as they used in my day. No one knew the old man. All the faces that I met were strange to me; some only bore a dim ghostly likeness to people I had known.

Once or twice Cuthbert told me the name of a passer-by, as we went along slowly under the lime-trees.

That was Jock Clifford's son, with the bat over his shoulder, a young man, fair and ruddy, but twice as old as his father was when I last saw him. From one of the cottages a child ran out, a brown-eyed toddling little girl, who came towards Cuthbert with a scream of pleasure, and called him grandfather. 'Our boy Will's little lass,' said Cuthbert, raising her on to his shoulder. He called to a woman passing by and bade her come and see an old friend. She came with the hesitating look of one who is told to speak to a stranger. 'You do not know him, Phillis,' Cuthbert said.

Was that Phillis, Hildred's little niece, the laughing rosy child that I remembered? Could this be her?

My heart failed me. The day that I belonged to had indeed passed away. I could not bear to see Hildred grown strange to me like the rest.

It was not that I should love the altered face less, far from it. But I had carried the young bright image of my one love for so long in my heart, I could not bear to lose it.

For those who lived with her, each line, each change, must have grown dear. To me they would be strange, and I feared lest afterwards I might never be able to call back again the gracious presence that had cheered my lonely life.

So, as twilight was over before we reached the Castle, I begged Cuthbert to leave me by the old well, and to bring Hildred to me there, that, in the darkness, I might hold her hand and hear her voice once more, then go my way, and still think of her without one shadow on her face that time or care had thrown.

Cuthbert, willing to do my pleasure though he but half understood me, obeyed my wish.

It was not for long that he left me alone, yet in those few minutes my whole life seemed to pass before me. Near me, above the well, were the old carved words of the promise I had once doubted. It had been too hard for me to make out when I was a child—it was too dark to read it now; yet even in this world it had been fulfilled. That cup of cold water given a life-time ago, had in no wise lost its reward. Cuthbert and Hildred had been happy. And for me, when I was left alone, God Himself drew nigh and was my Friend; though there had been some darkness on my way, the Light of lights, ever brightening, was shining on it.

Thinking thus, I saw that a figure came towards me swiftly through the darkness.

I took the hands she held out to me in my own, and heard her say, 'Willie, welcome home.'

Just for a few moments the weight of years was lifted off our heads, and Hildred and I were boy and girl once more.

We did not say much, nor did I stay long with her. I was content to have been near her, and to have listened to her voice. We parted presently, with a blessing spoken quietly, as befitted those who had once loved each other well, but whom God in His good providence had parted, and who never looked to meeting in this world again. And I went away.

So the two faces I have loved the most, Hildred's and my mother's, never grew old for me, but shine on me still, and are for ever young, for ever fair.

And I think that when I see them next they will be fairer yet, for they will have 'put on immortality.'

CONCLUSION.

Lead kindly Light, amid the encircling gloom,
Lead Thou me on.
The night is dark, and I am far from home,
Lead Thou me on.

O'er moor and fen, o'er crag and torrent, till
The night is gone,
And with the morn those angel faces smile,
Which I have loved long since, and lost awhile.

On the following morning Wandering Willie was astir betimes. He was bound for the farm-house where dwelt Roger's father—a good step, as he said to Lois, across the hills.

It was not snowing when he started. The morning clouds were even touched with red, but there were others hanging low down, grey clouds with wind-frayed edges, that looked heavy still with snow.

Lois went with the old man as far as the gate, over the path, where already, people coming and going, had beaten a track across the snow. There she parted from him.

'It makes me sad to see you going away alone,' she said, leaning over the gate, which he had already passed through, and holding his hand across it.

'It is good to be alone,' said Willie, quietly.

'But the journey will be so long—so toilsome.'

'Then, Lois, I shall sleep the sounder at the end,' answered the old man with a smile.

'Ah,' said Lois, 'you are tired already.'

'Already,' he repeated musingly. 'Am I *already* tired? Is it not nearly time for rest? Lois,' he went on, 'there was an old man who made a prayer once, and I think since then it has ever been the best-loved prayer of all the old and the weary. You know it?'

'I think I do,' said Lois.

'Yes, you know it well.' But still, as if he could not resist repeating the dear words, Willie uncovered his head, saying in an earnest voice, 'Lord, now lettest Thou Thy servant depart in peace, according to Thy word.' Then he turned to Lois with his child-like smile, and continued: 'I have prayed it so very often, Lois, that I sometimes think the answer must come soon.'

For a moment or two he still stood looking upward; afterwards, he bade farewell again to Lois.

And Lois, answering in the words she knew would please him best, said to him, 'Go in peace.'

She was glad that he left her with a smile—glad of the blessing he called down upon her head.

Watching him as he went away steadily, with his face turned towards the sun-rising, it seemed to Lois as if a rose-tinted morning cloud went with him and overshadowed him.

On the evening of the following day Roger's father rode up to the farm-house.

He brought tidings of wild weather out upon the moors, and told how he and his good horse had been more than once all but buried in a snow-drift.

'I should not have cared to come across on such a tempestuous day,' he added, 'only I want an answer, Roger, to my question.'

'But you got my answer, surely,' said Roger, quickly; 'Wandering Willie carried it to you yesterday.'

His father shook his head. 'Wandering Willie has not been nigh our place,' he said, in a marked, grave tone.

All looked at each other, but no one spoke, only Lois gave a low cry, 'Oh Willie, poor Willie!'

'Lois,' said Roger, coming to her side, 'trust us; we will do all we can—all that there is to do.'

Half-an-hour later every man about the farm went out into the darkness.

Lois, watching with her mother, saw her father go; Roger's father too—his long ride and his weariness quite forgotten. They walked with deliberate determined steps, and few words.

Far ahead already, Lois could just distinguish Roger—all the young men of the place following him—as he stood for a moment a dim figure against a dark sky. He disappeared, and Lois said in her heart, 'May God go with him.'

Three hours—four hours passed—they must be searching still! None of them returned that night.

About midnight the scattered groups of searchers met together.

It was a striking scene.

The setting moon, hung round with inky clouds, cast a pale glimmering of light down on to the snow. All round, the moors lay wild and tumbled, with black shadows here and there, cast by the waning moon.

It was cold, but intensely still, with a hush that gave an impression of breathless expectation.

For a little while the men stood together consulting. Then they separated again, Lois's father heading one party of searchers, while Roger went with the other.

All carried lanterns, and when they had gone a little way in their different directions, each, looking back towards the others, could only see a few shadowy figures gliding on into the darkness.

The night passed on. The moon set, and the hours of great darkness that came before the dawn had stolen upon them.

At last there came a shout from those a little way in front. The others hurried up. They had found footmarks in the snow. For a little time they followed them clearly; then they failed, for the wind had blown the snow wildly about, and had effaced them.

They dispersed once more, and searched eagerly and silently. By and by one of them called again. The footmark was found, and they never quite lost it afterwards. Sometimes it went straight forward for a little way, then it turned back over almost the same ground. Once or twice the steps crossed and recrossed each other. Often, from the marks in the snow, it seemed as if some one had stood still and waited, and turned this way and that, searching for the road.

Then they stood still too and shouted, calling the lost man's name. Again, and yet again. Strong men as they were, they shivered at the dead blank silence that was their only answer. No echo even, sent them back their voices.

The dawn was coming now, grey and chill, and there was a dull light on the snow. They began to see each other's anxious faces. Still they carried the lanterns low before them, and their great shadows followed weird behind.

The red lantern-light fell on the frozen foot-prints, one by one. They were easy to follow by this time. It must have ceased snowing before they were made, and the wind, too, must have gone down. They were deep and wavering now, as of one who walked heavily, dragging his steps wearily through the snow.

A little way off there was a hollow in the moor, a broken ridge of crags, and a huge stone, round one side of which the snow had drifted thickly. The footsteps ended there.

When the men reached the stone they stood still, but they raised no shout, though their search was over. Why was it that the voices which had been strained so often to reach the lost man's ears, were sunk to a low whisper now, that would not have roused a sleeping child?

Wandering Willie lay at their feet, his head resting on the snow-covered stone. One hand was underneath his head, the other had fallen by his side, and the staff lay close to it, just as the tired hand had laid it down.

They tried gently to raise that arm, but it was quite stiff, frozen into the snow. They laid their hands softly upon his heart, and it was perfectly still. Then they let the full light from the lanterns fall upon his face, and they saw that the old man looked utterly peaceful, nay, almost smiling, and that his eyes were closed.

His pack was unstrapped, and lay beside him on the snow. He had said to Lois that the toilsome journey would make him sleep all the sounder. Yes, so soundly that nothing earthly would awake him, ever any more.

As they stood round him silently, with bowed heads, the clouds parted in the east and the great sun rose up. The snow changed from dull grey to sparkling white, the clouds floated in rosy brightness, and the sun still rose until its clear red light streamed across Willie's face.

It was not hard to guess how it had been. The old man had found his way easily, as long as he kept upon the beaten path, but when he struck into the wild cross-track over the moor, the blinding mist and driving sleet bewildered him. The wind-driven snow drifted across the path and hid it, shrouding the familiar landmarks from his sight. It must have been as though a white mask lay over all the country.

Willie had never got very far. They thought he must have tried to turn back, but not until he had quite lost his way, and then the darkness came on. At last, perplexed and probably very weary, he had lain down to rest where the big stone sheltered him from the wind. After that he did not suffer any more. Sleep and death came to him quietly, hand in hand.

This was what Roger tried to tell Lois, when, going home before the others, he met her coming towards him along the road that led to the moor.

'Roger—well?'

'Dear Lois,' he said gravely and very tenderly, 'they are bringing him. I came on to tell you. He could not have suffered much.'

'Oh Roger, then he is dead!'

'Yes, Lois, yes. We found him lying on the snow, looking as if he had just fallen asleep.'

'Frozen to death. Oh, Roger—poor Willie!'

'Dearest,' he said, putting his arm round her, 'you would not cry if you had seen his face.'

'But such a lonely death!'

'He is glad now,' said Roger, with something like a sob.

Was it a lonely death? Who knows? It may be that, bearing the summons home, God had sent some messenger from the unseen world, who had been suffered to become a visible presence to the closing eyes. It may be that some voice—perhaps his mother's—had sounded once again in the ears, where its echo had lingered so long. We cannot tell.

Only no child's head was ever pillowed more peacefully in its dreamless sleep, than was Wandering Willie's, resting on the stone round which the snow had drifted.

And who, that looked into his restful face, could doubt that the old man's prayer was heard?

Down to the white moorland the Master sent at last, the message of recall, and hearing it even through the deep snow-sleep of that winter's night, His servant arose gladly, and from earth's storms and weariness he departed in peace.